The Wheel
of
God

by Arend Wieman

Printed in Victoria, Canada

National Library of Canada Cataloguing in Publication Data

Wieman, Arend
 The wheel of God
 ISBN 1-55212-919-5
 I. Title.
 PS8595.I53144W45 2001   C813'.54   C2001-902564-5
 PR9199.3.W478W45 2001

TRAFFORD

This book was published *on-demand* in cooperation with Trafford Publishing.
On-demand publishing is a unique process and service of making a book available for retail sale to the public taking advantage of on-demand manufacturing and Internet marketing.
On-demand publishing includes promotions, retail sales, manufacturing, order fulfilment, accounting and collecting royalties on behalf of the author.

Suite 6E, 2333 Government St., Victoria, B.C. V8T 4P4, CANADA
Phone   250-383-6864   Toll-free   1-888-232-4444 (Canada & US)
Fax   250-383-6804   E-mail   sales@trafford.com
Web site   www.trafford.com   TRAFFORD PUBLISHING IS A DIVISION OF TRAFFORD HOLDINGS LTD.
Trafford Catalogue #01-0321   www.trafford.com/robots/01-0321.html

10   9   8   7   6   5   4   3   2   1

Table of Contents

Chapter 1
The War After The War

Germany had lost the war, and to many of us young men who had served in any of the forces and were fortunate enough to make it home again in one piece, an almost hopeless, empty and sometimes terrible time followed. A war of a different kind seemed to hound us now like a faint shadow of a full moon during a cloudless night following the lonely wanderer in the field, and it could not be warded off with guns or other weaponry we soldiers had been trained to use. Yet, this conflict, this battle, was not less destructive to the human consciousness, and could be deadlier even to some of the old survivors of the war.

For seven years I had been in the German Air Force and now was confronted with a dreamless world, a hard and even hostile world, where other laws and rules were in place, and where we were manipulated by other standards in a cold and aimless society. The future looked as bleak as ... as the battlefield almost, the arena of action where we had faced death so many times and knew so well. But this time our comrades were missing, we stood on our own, lonely, individual selves.

I had to learn a brand new job to be able to provide for my family and myself. As young and as immature I was—and perhaps also to belong, to be loved in a cold war where nothing made sense anymore—I foolishly had married a girl of eighteen I had known for several months, and who later became the mother of my two daughters. Our union had very little to do with real love, a quality, an attribute I was not familiar with at the time and only connected

1

with sex.

Recently released from Russian prison, we had come from east Germany over an unknown frontier, drawn by the super-powers. Using the daring of my old profession and with a lot of luck, I was able to get us all into the west, in spite of my weak condition. We moved into the large twenty-eight-room house of my grandfather, also the home of my parents, my sisters, an aunt and some renters. But it soon became apparent that this was not going to be a peaceful life at all.

I was at odds with my father, who had been interned by the English for several months because of his Nazi activities. We had endless verbal arguments and fights over the past Hitler time and the lost war. Often our shouts could be heard through the whole house or across the large garden. I was at odds with my mother, who never lost an opportunity to meddle in my and our family life. And I also was at odds with my two sisters, who never had seen nor experienced any of the real war action—our little northwest German resort town was twenty or so miles from the nearest city where the severe bombing took place—nor did they want to know about it. We never could see eye to eye on anything concerning my family.

The only peaceful current in all those negative vibrations was my grandfather. He never involved himself in our arguments and conflicts, and often enough wasn't even aware of them. I would inherit the house from him, which was an eyesore to my mother, because her daughters were much more suited to take over the place, for reasons I never was able to establish.

My aunt had died of cancer shortly after our arrival. When my grandfather died at the ripe old age of eighty-eight years, and I shortly thereafter discovered that I had been tricked out of my inheritance, our conflicts became almost unbearable. Although my family and I now were living in a separate part of the house, away from my mother and sisters, and I had started a radio store with an old friend as a partner, I seriously considered to get out of this whole... unhealthy atmosphere. I longed for peace in more than one way!

In the summer of 1952, my family and I emigrated to Alberta, Canada, to the city of Edmonton, to begin a new life. I had learned a new trade, that of an electrician, and was very confident I would find a job soon with that kind of occupation. I was hired by an aircraft repair company.

2

Although we had to work hard to make ends meet, particularly because of our limited English language, one should think that the New World would bring us happiness and contentment. But not so! The war we had tried to leave behind, continued. Looking back today, I freely admit that the main reason for the continuation of the conflicts was myself because of my immaturity, my bossiness and my general concept of how we should constitute our life.

The stubborn self-righteousness on my part created endless frictions, if not too serious at first. Then, adding to this, a deep down feeling of helplessness in our new country perhaps also began to magnify the insecurity of our relationship. Although some inter and outer play was to be expected with young and inexperienced people like us, and we would have survived these marital troubles if it weren't for my unbending and childish outlook and my consciousness in general. I had known the hard life of a soldier and did not know how to convert to this different world; I did not know how to bend a little here and there, and tolerance, humility and love were strangers to me.

Well, our marriage went broke after many painful years of trying it again. My wife married another, much older man eventually and found happiness. But our daughters still had to suffer, being torn back and forth between their parents. I found it extremely difficult to cut the deep emotional bonds I had with my children, which effected them negatively right into their adult years, when they started their own family lives. For myself, I kept on struggling with this abnormal emotional link until much later.

When I moved to the west coast of British Columbia finally, this bond with my daughters weakened considerably, severed by the distance between us to a certain extent. For me it would become a vastly different life in every aspect and from every point of view. This new environment would make a new man out of me, a new human being.

Almost immediately, I noticed that the people were different in their conduct and relationships. They appeared to be more open and happier. Because I liked this so vary different spirit, I opened to it and it began to reflect on my inner being. I was easily led and even bent, knowing that it was for my betterment and also to have relief from my old pains.

Still immature in many ways, however, I had several agonizing disappointments, created by myself mostly; with a childish abstinence, I bluntly refused to look behind the scenes of life.

I found a job again as an aircraft electrician and thrived on my work. The very first money I was able to save, I used as a down-payment for a medium-sized house. I converted it into a duplex, to live in one part myself and rent out the other.

But not too long hence a city inspector appeared, telling me in no uncertain terms that I needed an outside fire escape from the upstairs rooms. He must have nudged some of his peers at city hall because others came to tell me that the plumbing and electrical wiring needed overhauling and repair. And then, to put the finishing touches to my anger, one of these fellows told me that the old basement had to be properly lined with cement.

Well, the anger went, fear took hold and I lost my head. Before all this really got out of hand—more likely, though, I was not able to deal with the situation and that of the adult world—I immediately sold the place again to the lady I had bought it from to begin with. My short-lived dream, to buy another house every year with a down payment, and to live off the rent of a dozen of them eventually—happily ever after—had burst like a soap bubble. I still had this 'get rich quickly' idea in my system, something I had brought with me from the Old Country. After all—an inner voice was telling me—this was Canada with endless resources and possibilities, and I was a smart opportunist who had everything in the palm of my hand. Unfortunately, I was the kind who only would learn out of hard experiences.

Slowly, very slowly, my consciousness changed and began to soften; I became more aware of the virtues of life and, to give one example, that there was something beside and beyond wanting, namely giving.

The coast, with the many different kinds of people, opened other avenues to me also, like the occult, the metaphysics, the mysteries and, not to forget, the flying saucers. More and more books on these subjects began to line the shelves of my little suite. I became fascinated with reincarnation; that we should've lived many other lifetimes before, going back thousands of years on the time track? I began to have vivid dreams and started to record them in a dream journal. It simply was too interesting, too intriguing and too vast in scope to be left in the past, never to be remembered again. At this moment I did not know how to interpret some of the dreams properly; perhaps later I would be more knowledgeable and their meaning might give me a deeper insight into my life.

One day—it was during a lunch break at work—I heard my fellow electricians speaking about a farm with a house and forty acres for sale. The father of one of them had died and now they found it hard to get rid of the place because it happened to be at the end of a road, about an hour's drive from Vancouver. Immediately I sharpened my ears, and I had a nudge from the inside. Was this something I should be interested in? At quitting time I approached the fellow worker, and asked if I could see the farm. All afternoon certain thought had manifested in my mind and now I had the distinct desire to follow them through.

It was an old place all right, but all the buildings were of a solid structure, if old fashioned. Most of the land was unkept with the exception of a good-sized garden. I could see rolling hills almost all around, hiding the place even from the next-door neighbor, a half-mile back down the road. I saw the Rocky Mountains in the distance, though.

The only way I can describe my reaction is that I was instantly in love with the farm and I wanted it. They asked for cash and I had no difficulties getting the money from the bank. In a day I owned the place and was very happy.

The house had two bedrooms, a kitchen, a living and utility room and two more empty rooms that hadn't seen any life or a dust cloth for many years. The dug-out basement harbored a nearly new oil-wood heater. There also was enough room for plenty of storage with a direct door to the outside.

Besides the very roomy barn and chicken coop, there were five other outbuildings, all in good shape. I particularly liked the large pond beside the fenced-in garden. I was thinking of a little boat and some ducks for my leisurely past-time and interludes. Yes, this place in the country sat right with me; it no doubt would change my consciousness for the better in more ways than one.

Chapter 2

Lingering Imprints Prevail

My father was born in the country, the third of five children, and since only the oldest boy could inherit the farm, he was sent off to become a teacher. Although he studied in German, French and English universities and went through every phase of the first World War, he never was able to detach himself from his beloved soil; with his emotions he stayed close to the land. However, he expected everybody else also to feel his way.

Since our own sizeable garden was not large enough for his farming in miniature, he rented another piece of land a half mile away, to dig, to plant and to harvest. And who was to be his helper? It was his son, naturally. Early as a boy he employed me already, and every year I disliked it more until I hated it. Gardening was not what I was born for. My stars had put me in harmony with everything technical. I loved to invent and my head was full of all kinds of gadgets I wanted to build, if I only had the means and the time. I never got past building airplane models, though. Most of them flew very well, considering that I didn't use any plans, as the others boys did so diligently.

* * *

This desire of wanting to invent I was not able to tuck away in all those years; it continued simmering in my subconscious mind, only to burst forth if the first opportunity should present itself.

Suddenly now, without having had lingering thoughts on the

subject of invention, this opportunity tabled itself like a rabbit out of a magician's hat. As soon as I became aware of this fact, it kind of stunned me for a moment; it appeared so instant. My former urge of wanting to invent—to manifest something of my own creation—had made a giant leap from my boyhood days to the present; absolutely nothing would deter me anymore now.

To begin with, I converted the barn into a workshop. The old workbench was rough but good enough for the time being. Naturally, I also adopted the old tools I had inherited with the place and added some electrical equipment. I also created a special corner where I would do some work in electronics, my big love.

The thought that I could be technically creative, unlimited, do what I wanted, gave me almost an ecstatic feeling, as if a floodgate of my consciousness had been opened. This part of my inner self had been restrained far too long.

* * *

First, however, I would have to put my attention on the garden the farmer had put in already before he died. Would I put some of my labor into working the soil? In reflecting on the matter, I discovered that my hatred had vanished; after all, the garden was there and I intended to get some fresh vegetables on the table. I could see it so clearly now that my ardent dislike for 'working the land', as my dad had called it lovingly, was originated in the fact that I had been pressured into doing it. Having the freedom today of doing my own choosing, created no such … negative feelings.

I had no clue as to what the former owner—who had been a very old man of over ninety—had planted already. All I could see were several rows of plants poking their heads through the soil. So I had to wait and see what else the garden eventually produced.

To beautify the immediate surroundings, I bought several flowers, though. There were hundreds of snowdrops and crocuses all over; their prime time had passed already. Every house window had a flower box, and I did them all with fresh soil and put in my favorite flowers of nasturtiums, sweet peas, pansies, besides tulips, hyacinths and narcissus.

I think that for the first time in my life I was able to put some kind of love into what I was doing because it involved my heart. This realization startled me at first; had I missed out on love in all my living years? Perhaps I had. In the past I had connected love with something physical and not with the heart.

7

It gave me a good feeling that I could call something my home now; here I was the only one involved and it felt right to the inner being, I was very happy.

When I began to develop some intestine trouble, it came as a total surprise to me. What in the world could cause this sickness? I kept on asking myself. Finally I decided to see a doctor. He told me to relax and take a long holiday. I had worried too much and it had created an imbalance in my system, as colitis was the result.

I honestly did not understand the doctor's advice because I was happy, liked my work as an aircraft electrician and certainly was not under any stress. On the contrary, I never before had felt so contented in my life. So I saw another doctor, and another and... Well, after five more of them and a lot of double-talk, demonstrating some kind of pity for me and a lot of prescriptions for pills and medicine, I finally came to an old and wise physician. He knew pretty well what had happened and that I had come to a stage of distrust in the medical profession because of his peers' limited and often controversial advice in my particular disorder. He quickly judged me correctly to be an unorthodox individual who needed special handling and healing.

Instead of giving me the usual talk and resume, he simply had a friendly chat with me, mostly not even related to my intestine trouble. I had told him my love for reading, so he gave me a book written by a doctor—an exceptional psychiatrist, as I discovered much later while reading it—and advised me to read other literature also, writing down a list of books. He never gave me the feeling of inferiority and I felt to be on even terms with him. Much later I began to realize that this knowledgeable old-ager wanted me to discover on my own what was wrong with me and why. One out of six doctors who was able to come across to my particular malady, which involved my emotions and mind much more than my physical parts.

After doing a lot of reading I decided to become my own physician. I realized that deep down I had been, and still was, partly a worrier. The main reason had been my daughters, that I had not been able to give them a proper home, a proper upbringing with both parents. This worry had anchored itself in the crevices of my subconscious mind to be manifested now physically in my intestine, a fact I found extremely hard to believe at first. But, through reading the right literature, I discovered it on my own, which made it so valuable to me. I was the kind of a person who only found real value in self-discovery.

Well, many other avenues were opened to me at the same time, some related to psychiatry, nutrition and nature in general. I learned about organic gardening and its value to sensitive people like myself. My consciousness experienced an enormous growth. Completely new sciences were born I never believed existed, and I began to love them.

I never stopped wondering, though, why I was so terribly sensitive now. After all, I had gone through the war with all the killings and cruelties, and hardly had experienced any scratch on the physical level. To put some light into all this, I was taken one night in my dream beyond the scenes of life into the far reaches of soul's existence.

* * *

"So you want to know where and how your present sensitivity started?" I thought I heard a voice asking me. It was not a voice in the sense that I heard it in words; it was an impression rather. This dream master was familiar to me, I recognized him as an old acquaintance, not that I ever had seen him personally. This was a dream experience where no interpretation was necessary.

It began in England, shortly before the second Crusade was just about to be launched in France and Germany. With the blessings of his parents, young Conrad sailed across the English Channel for France to the castle of his father-in-law, the Baron de Troxeau, because he wanted to join the army of knights and soldiers who soon would be marching to the Holy Land.

* * *

Pope Eugenius had asked King Louis VII of France, to help the Christians who lived in Jerusalem and the surroundings, because the Turks were on the verge of driving them out.

What the Pope did not want to happen, namely to start another Holy War, materialized just the same. The disaster and misfortune of the first Holy War, only forty-five years before, already had been forgotten. The knights and soldiers were hungry for action; they had been out of jobs for too long. Inevitably, the call by the Pope avalanched into the second Crusade.

It took over a year to ready for the Holy Land adventure and King Louis of France personally would lead his army and the many private citizens who craved to visit Christ's place of action

9

and death. The arduous and tragic march began in 1144 A.D., and was joined by the Germans, who went ahead.

* * *

All this happening had flashed in a few seconds through my consciousness and I became aware of the fact that I was young Conrad in that lifetime. I listened to the highly emotional discussions and arguments at the castle of my father-in-law. My hot-tempered uncles left no doubt what their intentions were and did not heed the warnings of the old soldiers who still were remembering the last tragedy only too well. And that included me, because my passions were running too high to have any reasonable thoughts come to the surface.

Although twenty-two years of age, my physical stature was not of the strongest to be a knight, but I was an expert shot with the crossbow and handled the lighter weaponry well. Back home in England, my experienced father had given me an excellent training.

Our spirits were high, when we finally began the long march southeast, and nobody thought in negative terms. We lived off the land and often enough farms and towns were ransacked for food, but possessions also; those times were heartless, indeed.

At Constantinople, King Louis was advised by Emperor Manuel of Byzantium, to bypass the city and take a different route from the Germans. However, the King did not trust the Emperor and marched right through the city. Here the German strays joined us and their hair-raising stories of misadventure and loss of many lives should have been a blow to all of us, including the King. But, unfortunately, ignorance and arrogance were only too often the companions of chivalry.

After having crossed the Straits to Asia Minor, our march became a terrible hardship. In the coastal rocky hills we were continuously harassed and attacked by local tribes and many of our civilian followers lost their possessions and, often enough, their lives also. The behavior of the knights particularly was terrible to watch, the way they only thought of themselves and repeatedly tortured and killed captured women and children. When I approached one of my uncles about it, he kicked me several times and shouted me out of his tent under everybody's laughter.

Now I seriously began to wonder about the honesty of our mission. The King knew of all the going-ons and didn't do

10

anything about it. Suddenly I found myself in the throngs of a hopeless situation I was not able to get out of. Desperately, I tried to shield my ears from the screams of the poor people and ignore the way they were mishandled and killed by the so-called liberators of the Christians and the Holy Land. It was utterly impossible, though, and it effected my inner being terribly.

Arriving in Antioch, we rested for a while until King Louis heard that the German Emperor already had made it to Jerusalem. This was something unbearable to him. Consequently, he rushed us on down south and we all crammed into Jerusalem for several months. Day and night everybody quarreled with each other, our French soldiers with the Germans, the Germans with the Germans and the French with the French.

Finally it was decided to attack Damascus, even though this was a neutral city. But they only were thinking of booty and the spoils to be had there. However, this was a very big city indeed, and there were not enough men to handle a siege of any length of time.

It soon looked as if the Emir of Damascus wanted to teach us, the so-called Crusaders, a good lesson. Slowly and surely, we were driven back to Jerusalem. Hundreds of us were killed by skilled horsemen and bowmen, dashing in and out of our marching columns. It took a good week to get back to the Holy City, in very bad shape.

In disgust, the German Emperor packed up, leaving his troops and people behind, trying to make it back to Germany on his own. Unfortunately, though, our French King was too stubborn, he would not admit defeat.

For me it had been all too much, I was not able to cope any longer with my emotional pains and distress; I had a nervous breakdown and went into a coma. It was a wonder that I survived. Regaining consciousness, I discovered that I was very weak and had lost control over my bowels, right arm and leg.

With a caravan we wounded and disabled were sent to the Mediterranean Sea. At Acree they loaded us on two ships for Italy. But it was the time of the winter storms and both ships with all of us aboard sank. There were no survivors.

* * *

With a strong jolt I woke up, kind of catapulting me back to the present. For a long time I lay awake, going over that dramatic dream experience again, until the light of dawn finally reminded me where I was now. Before breakfast I had the whole dream written down in my dream journal. This was something I would not so quickly forget again, that the weakness of my intestine today should have originated several lifetimes and centuries ago in this Holy Land venture I participated in. It opened another chapter of my past, exposing vital imprints of my karma I had brought with me into this life.

Chapter 3
Young Friends – Old Relations

Looking at the chicken coop one day, I decided to repair it and get me some feather friends so I could enjoy fresh eggs. I also bought a rooster, because in one of the health books the doctor spoke of the value of fertilized eggs; besides I liked the crowing early in the morning. When the chickens began to lay and produced too many eggs for my own consumption, I took them to work where my fellow workers gladly took them off my hands for a dollar a dozen.

My head was so full of all the things I wanted to build and invent, that I did not know with what to begin.

It was a beautiful morning on a sunny Saturday and I had the large barn doors of my workshop wide open to let the fresh and warm air flood around me. This was perfect to do some thinking, as I remember so vividly my grandfather doing it when I was a small boy. He usually sat in front of his workbench, his legs crossed and swinging the upper one continuously. I like to position my legs high up while sitting in an easy chair and get my mind to work and be creative, often moving my hands behind my head or folding them on my chest.

Suddenly I had the feeling of being watched. Without moving my head too much, I let my eyes wander around and soon discovered two pairs of eyes through the wide hinch-opening of one of the door halves. The heads pulled back when they thought that I had glimpsed into their direction. Out of the corner of my eyes I saw the heads moving back slowly into the spacious door slot again. With an inner grin and looking in the opposite direction I called out, "You may come in, children, I don't mind."

A girl and a boy slowly came around the door, moving reluctantly toward me. I turned around with my swivel chair, smiled warmly at them and asked, "Who are you?"

"I'm Hanna and this is Willy," the girl answered, pointing at the boy.

I grinned and asked, "Willy and Hanna who?"

"I'm Willy Hillard," the boy said rather quickly with some discomfort.

Coming a step forward, the girl said assured, as if I should have known, "I'm Hanna Bonson."

"Ah, you're one of the five Bonson children," I smiled, "so I finally meet you personally." I motioned toward a bench invitingly and said, "Please sit down, you two."

The Bonsons were my next door farmers and lived a half a mile down the road. I had spoken with the parents, Marg and Bill, a couple of times, but only had seen their five children fleetingly. I guessed them to be between ten and seventeen years of age.

Putting my feet on the floor I bent forward to turn the radio on because it was the time for my favorite music over this particular station. I then asked, "What kind of music do you like?"

"We can only listen to what mom and dad play; that old stuff, you know," the girl answered. "Kind of what you play now."

"And you, Willy?" I asked the boy.

He still wasn't too comfortable, but answered, "I haven't got a radio and my mother puts on records and tapes when she comes home from work or has a visitor."

To put him more at ease I asked, "What can I do for you two? I suppose you're looking for a job?"

While the boy only nodded, Hanna said, "Yeah; you have some, Mister Hellmer?"

I put a hand on my chin, indicating that I was trying to think of something. Then I beckoned them to follow me out of the barn. We walked toward the pond, the fenced-in garden and the nearby chicken coop. I said, "It looks pretty rough all around hear, doesn't it? It needs cutting all right. I've an old mower, but it doesn't run. What do you say if we repair it first, hey?"

We pulled the old machine out of one of the outbuildings and rolled it into my workshop. I asked, "What's usually the first thing one looks for, if it doesn't want to start?"

14

"The sparkplug," Hanna called out. "We always help dad."

"Right!" I gave her credit. Under their observing eyes I took the sparkplug out and showed it to them. "What do you think?" I asked.

They both raised their shoulders, clearly not knowing what to look for. So I explained it to them. "See, it's all gummed up and you can't even see the gap anymore." I fastened it into the vice and began to clean it with a steel brush, while explaining. "That's how it's supposed to look, nice and clean. This gap here is much too wide, so we just give it a little tap to narrow it; see? I bet that the gas line is all fouled up, too, and we better clean the carburetor also. I want you to know all this, so you can do it next time without my help."

I gave them the jobs to wash and clean the different parts in a bath of diesel fuel with a brush and in one and a half hours we had it all together again. I asked them, "You think it'll run now?"

"I'll bet it does," Hanna called out. She obviously was the talker.

After the third pull on the rope, which had to be inserted anew on top of the flywheel every time, it began to sputter, until the run became very smooth. We three were very satisfied with ourselves.

I said, "Now then, you two better remember that we only can use this oil and gas mixture for that little motor. Straight gas will be fatal, it'll burn the motor very quickly. Okay? They both nodded, and I added, "On the car, as you know, the gas and oil are used separately."

"Now, let's have a look at the blade," I said, turning the mower over. "Terrible; see that? There's not much of a cutting edge left; we better sharpen it good."

After another half an hour on the electric grindstone, we finally had the mower ready to be used. "Okay, you guys, I only want you to cut the grass around the pond and the garden-chicken area," I said, "the rest stays wild as it is. Now then, how much are you going to charge me for an hour?"

They looked at each other and raised their shoulders. I probably was their first customer and would be the only one, living right here at the end of the road. There were no other neighbors in a two-mile range.

So I suggested, "How about a dollar each, and you come back every two or three weeks, as long as it keeps on growing in spring,

15

summer and fall?"

The way the two went to work, with the enthusiasm, it was apparent to me, that they never had worked for anybody and certainly not for money. Nice kids, I liked them. I brought them a couple of rakes and just put them into the grass without saying anything. Seeing it from the distance they raised a hand and nodded, indicating that they had understood, namely to rake the grass up after they were finished.

Suddenly, I became aware of the fact that it was already past lunch time and we had been too busy to notice. I went into the house and made some sandwiches for the two. Together with a jug of juice, I brought them out to the children and placed them on a bench at the pond. I called out, "Lunch time, you two, come and get it!" They shut the motor off and came running, while I walked back to the house, grinning with satisfaction.

Well, I didn't have to coax them to do other little jobs for me here and there, and we three got along just fine. Our relationship developed into a warm friendship. More and more the children became attracted to and interested in the things I wanted to invent and was working on. Often it was a lot of fun with us and we had many laughs together if something didn't work as we expected it, or if it simply worked like a charm. There were times when I was amazed over both of their understandings and even solid suggestions they made. After all, they were only children of eleven years of age and never had been trained in technical matters.

* * *

Driving home from work one evening, Marg Bonson stopped me at their house and invited me in for a chat. It soon became apparent that she wanted to know whether Hanna and her friend, Willy, were any bother?

"Not at all, Marg," I set her mind to rest in putting assurance into my words. "You don't know how much I enjoy them. Why, what did they tell you?"

"Oh, we just wanted to make sure. I mean, they eat with you and all that," Marg went on. "You know how kids are at times. And I better tell you, with Willy, there is no father, you know, and she works and often isn't at home on evenings to look after the boy. We are not quite sure what's going on there ... Maybe there are other men, you know what I mean? There are times when Willy looks very tired ... we can't get anything out of him and ...

16

well, what else can we do?"

I nodded. "I see what you mean. Thanks for telling me. I always wanted to ask you. You see, on weekends I'm there and we three are such good friends that ... I kind of thought whether I should ask them to stay overnight. I've the big house all to myself with plenty of rooms and beds, and ... if I have your permission? But I would have to phone his mother, too, of course, to get her permission. Or it might even be better to see her personally, if you have her address."

Marg answered, "We have nothing against Hanna staying over, Arden, but the boy? I don't know. It might be an idea to see what she's like, you know what I mean. Sometimes we feel that the boy needs help, but, you can't interfere..."

I nodded, while Marg got up, jotting down the address and telephone number of Willy's mother. I am sure glad that we had that talk.

On my way from work, I rode past Willy's house, but it appeared that nobody was home, until one Sunday when I had been for a long ride over the country, to see something different away from my place. There was a car parked in front of the house and I heard loud music through an open window, so I stopped and knocked on the door. I waited at least a couple of minutes and knocked again, harder this time. Finally, a woman opened the door, and I said, "I wonder whether I could have a talk with you ... It's Mrs. Hillard, isn't it? My name is Arden Hellmer. It's about Willy..."

That's as far as I got and she burst out: "I know Willy got himself into a jam, I know it." She led me into the house.

After we had taken a seat in her living room, I said as calm as I could, "No, Mrs. Hillard, there is nothing wrong with Willy," I put emphasis on every word. "As far as I am concerned, he is a nice boy."

She acted surprised and asked, "Are you the police?"

"No, I'm not from the police at all," I replied very composed. "You see, Willy visits me occasionally with his friend, Hanna. You probably know the Bonsons. I'm their neighbor and live at the end of the road. Well, the kids and I have become good friends. They help me here and there and I was thinking, whether I should let them stay over on weekends. You have nothing to worry about, I had my own daughters, so I know about kids. I've the

17

Bonson's permission already. I though to see you personally, so you could see for yourself whether I'm trustworthy, you know what I mean?"

Obviously she was not prepared for anything of this nature, I could see that. She raised her shoulders and made a funny face, as if she couldn't care less. "Sure, why not. But throw him out if he is too much of a bother. You can give me a ring first. You mean, for two nights?"

I nodded, 'Yes.'

Suddenly her tune had a joyful sound to it when she said, "You can have him every weekend, then I don't have to be here at all. My work, you know."

When the Bonsons heard my story, Marg said. "I expected something similar. The boy needs help, I can see that. Well, we do what we can. We'll give him our love, that's what he needs most of all. What do you think, Bill?" she asked her husband.

Bill Bonson was rather the quiet type and he just raised his shoulders and eyebrows. So Marg continued, "I'm glad you went, Arden. I wonder where the boy was when you visited her? He wasn't here on that Sunday." Finally, she said with a deep breath, "Together we'll do our best."

* * *

I became aware of being a teacher in a large class of only boys. I was teaching mathematics on some technical data. The boys' age was about from ten to fourteen years. All were extremely attentive of what I had to say. Suddenly I realized that I was lecturing over a problem I had had my mind on for quite a long time, yet, here I was passing it on in all details, very much assured about the subject matter.

My awareness most of the time was that of the teacher, but in some moments of only seconds I was above the situation it seemed. In one of those instances, two of the students' faces passed my inner vision; I had Hanna (as a boy) and Willy in my class.

The lecture of the class went on for quite a while with many questions asked and answered. Only when I awoke then around two o'clock in the morning, did I realize that it had been a dream. It made me wide awake and I got up to write it immediately in my dream journal. I also made extensive notes over this technical data I had been teaching.

Later I must have fallen asleep again, because I had another dream. This one was in the south of Germany in the sixteenth century, which was impressed upon me. I was then the elder brother of twin boys, and very clearly I recognized Hanna and Willy out of our present lifetime in them. So we three had been together already in that incarnation, and Hanna as a boy again, as in the first dream.

I know in what country we were because we spoke German and the mighty Alp mountains in the background indicated the location. Our house had been rolled over only a few weeks earlier by an avalanche; both of our parents had been inside and were killed. As a young man of eighteen years I had to be mother and father to my little brothers of only five.

The dream was cut off rather quickly. I woke up wet with sweat, because during the dream I had been struggling up a steep hill to one of our higher pastures. The whole work of our little farm had been solely on my shoulders then.

* * *

All morning at work, my mind tried to digest the two dreams. Obviously, important messages were passed on to me. I understood the second dream only too well; it was self-evident, namely that the two children and I knew each other in that life in Germany already and why we three got along so well now.

However, there was a deeper meaning in that dream message also, in some way related to our relationship of today. Again, I was the older person, the teacher, the father figure, to Willy at least, and much was expected of me, so I believed.

I was at a loss with the first dream, though, what it might signify. We all wore tunics, as they had dressed in ancient Greece and Rome. But I was overwhelmed, to say it very mildly, by the advanced technical data I had been teaching, which I remembered very well and intended to use in one of my inventions.

At that time in my life, I was not experienced enough to interpret dreams like these, nor did I know too much of the spiritual worlds and the esoteric in general. Today I know that this experience had been in the Astral world; this fact escaped me completely at that moment in time. Most of us spend many earth years in between our physical lifetimes in an Astral environment, where a lot of schooling goes on, or one even holds a teaching position, as it was in my case. Over most of these lives in the

19

Astral worlds is a curtain drawn, of course, and the very same is the case with our past lives here on earth. None of them are remembered, unless a dream master finds it necessary to reveal one or another for reasons unknown to most of us in our limited consciousness.

* * *

When I saw my young friends the next weekend, naturally, I tried not to let on of what I knew about our past now. One thing I was very sure of, though, and that was that I never could see our relationship in the same light again. However, I would not devolve to them what I knew, it had to stay as my secret for a long time to come.

Chapter 4

A Real Mexican Treat

The healing of my inflamed large intestine moved along very slowly and I began to wonder what else I could do beside improving my food intake, swallow vitamins and thinking positive. It seemed to me that my guts were irritated by some foods more than by others, naturally or organically grown or not.

When I had the disappointing experience with the medical profession in the beginning and proclaimed that I would become my own doctor, I thought it would be easy to read a couple of dozen books and look after myself. What I didn't know then was that all of medicine is so vast, so multilateral, that not even a hundred university trained doctors would be able to master all of the different fields; certainly not just one person. Of course, this is not aimed to find an excuse for the physician's behavior toward me several months ago.

In any case, I had to admit now that I was stuck with my knowledge. The trouble was, though, which physician should I go to? There had not been many practitioners in the 1960s and early '70s who were very knowledgeable about nutrition, not to mention the immune system and allergies. The concept of Orthomolecular Medicine was hardly in its infancies at that time.

I had read about spas in Europe where I might have found some help and faster healing because the medical profession there was more open-minded and way ahead in natural healing methods, using mineral baths, fasting and juice diets. But I could not afford to go there; those places were too expensive for my wallet. However, I had read extensively about the papaya melon and the healing effects it might have on people with my plight.

21

When a health resort in Guadalajara, Mexico, advertised in a magazine I was reading, that this particular papaya diet was a specialty there, I decided to go and get myself healed, once and for all.

It was June already and I hated to leave my garden and the chickens, but, fortunately, I had the Bonsons as neighbors. Their oldest daughter, Helen, would look after my place. Besides, the two children would continue coming on weekends and do their jobs. Of course, I invited them all to stay overnight and sleep at my house if they so desired.

After I had told the doctor at work what my trouble was, I had no difficulty getting four weeks off. So one early morning, Helen Bonson took me to the airport and I was on my way to the sunny south for a very enlightened episode on all levels of human endeavor and adventure.

Although Guadalajara is over a mile above sea level, I was engulfed by hot air when I stepped off the plane in the evening. A taxi brought me the thirty or so miles out to the resort in the dark. Even in the headlights I could not fail to see that the country was very arid, because boulders and stones were strewn all over and the tree and vegetable growth was limited. Properties were divided by stone walls rather than by wood fences.

As soon as we had driven through the gate, the first thing I was told as a newcomer that there would be no smoking; away from that I was free to do my own thing. I doubled up with an old fellow in a large room and found it almost too hard to believe when he told me that he was already in his nineties. Well, there were many other surprises awaiting me.

As an early riser I walked and discovered the beautiful surroundings at dawn and came to a little pool where I took a swim. "His" and "Hers" indicated that one also could do some sunbathing behind the walls. While floating lazily in the water I listened to strange tropical bird voices and songs and some of them seemed to build their nests in a nearby banana tree.

At breakfast I was introduced to many other guests, almost all Americans and Canadians. During my stay I only encountered two Mexicans. The food was strictly vegetarian with the exception of eggs. I never saw so many different tropical fruits presented at every meal, but there also were plenty of a variety of vegetables, nuts, seeds, clabbered milk and many different freshly made juices. Papaya and garlic were strongly emphasized. I always began with a large glass of papaya juice and it became my staple with everything I ate. Loaded with enzymes, the papaya is an excellent predigestant and does wonders for people with a sluggish intestine. Some people had to have their eggs, toast and coffee for breakfast, and they were about the only ones catered to.

Later in the day I discovered that there also were yoga classes twice a day and I added those exercises to my daily agenda. To my utter amazement I soon learned that all the guests, without any exceptions, were interested in and even involved with flying saucers, the esoteric and related subjects. I even spoke with people who had been 'picked up by a large flying saucer for a space visit'. One engineer had been taken aboard a huge space vehicle and, there, technical problems were explained to him that he had been working on.

There were lectures twice a day by professional scientists and physicians, who happened to be at the resort as guests as I was, keeping me busy recording the many things I heard in a special journal. Later on then, I would be able to draw from this knowledge at home and utilize it as I saw fit.

I had endless suggestions and advice for my intestine condition. There were eight visiting medical practitioners, besides the two doctors who worked for the spa, seeking enlightenment on physical, mental and spiritual levels as much as the rest of us did. However, their discourses over often unorthodox medical practices and many different healing methods kept me on my toes and in awe. Their farsighted insight into medical matters was priceless. If only the rest of the medical men of this world would display this kind of open-mindedness and tolerance.

There was so little discontentment, so little negativity among the fifty guests, that one could think an invisible and godlike hand had put us together at the resort for a purpose. Although our beliefs, religions, philosophies, opinions and concepts of life were often vastly different, tolerance, acceptance and love overcame our differences.

In about two weeks time it had become apparent that my colitis – after talking with some of the doctors, I had my doubts that it actually was rightly diagnosed – had disappeared, and my strength picked up. No doubt the papaya and the raw fruit and vegetables were the reason.

Having been born and raised in a spa (bath) in Germany, I was very much aware of the value of mineral springs. In this Mexican location every water was hot, and one easily was able to boil an egg where the water gushed out of the rock wall. They actually had to drill for cold water and it was scarce, so that hot water was even used for the toilets.

I bathed every day once or twice and there was a bunch of us walking a mile down the river, where it was cool enough to swim, and let the healing minerals penetrate our skin. Not yet had the owner of the resort evaluated this element of the healing department. He advertised the papaya diet and its healing properties, a very substantial factor indeed.

My mind and journal were crammed with much new information for later use and evaluation at home. Shortly before my four weeks were up, I had a long six-hour hike on my own, because I was simply not able to find anybody who was willing to make this endurance diagnosis and test with me. Physically, I felt so on top of the world that I simply wanted to prove to myself how well I could do in a real challenge to mind and body. It was more of climbing and descending up and down rocky hills and mountains than anything else. When I came home in the late afternoon, I could've walked another six hours; my hike of endurance and challenge to the self had not been much of a confrontation, after all, but I was not disappointed.

In the truest sense of the word I had gone through a rejuvenation process and felt like twenty-five years old again; in fact, in some respects I felt better. I certainly had more endurance than during my early times as a youngster, when I was extensively involved in track and field and did a lot of training.

How could I help asking myself the question many times over, how this feat was possible? I also discussed it with two of the physicians and we came to the conclusion that beside the papaya diet with the fresh juices, my participation in the yoga exercises twice a day, my bathing in the hot springs, the thin air in the high altitude of over a mile above sea level, and, finally, the positive group attitude and its vibrations had contributed to my extraordinary physical well-being and healthful condition. Not many of the other guests had stuck it out as strictly and arduously as I had and certainly not many had been willing to participate in the daily yoga practices or even sit in the many hot water tubs, located in front of every building for some mineral absorption. To most of the people it had been a lazy holiday and only a few had come to find their health back as I did.

We hated to leave and part and say good-bye to each other. Although more than half had booked for six or even eight weeks of stay, when the first began to pack and leave, it developed into something like an avalanche. Again I had this feeling of an invisible hand at work behind the scenes. Whatever, the health resort of <u>Rio Caliente</u>, had left deep impressions on all levels of my being.

* * *

On my way home I stopped over in Los Angeles to visit a clinic and laboratory a bit north of there. Here I expected to get my blood tested for allergies, a science only recently developed by that physician into an art so exact that even the smallest allergy could be detected. Fortunately, one of the doctors at the resort had known about this and given me the address.

Well, it hardly took half a day to get my results back and discover that I had a long list of allergies. All my favorite foods were irritants to my system, like wheat, all dairy products, eggs, beef, chicken and several vegetables and fruits. I had to give up my beloved onions and garlic for the time being. The doctor emphasized to me to stay off all the allergy foods for some three months, to give the immune system the opportunity to repair itself and heal. After that time I could add these annoying foods again every four or five days only, without doing much harm.

This discovery of the relationship between the immune system and allergy foods was so brand new, that I was practically one of the first patients it was passed on to. They would have liked to keep me there or nearby at least to check the results. I promised them, though, to write occasional letters for their records. At least, there were no drugs involved in this method and one could rest assured.

* * *

On the last leg of my flight I felt jubilant; I would bring more than a handful of treasures home. I was thinking of the children, there would be so much to pass on to them.

Helen waited at the airport in Vancouver with my car and she was telling me all the news on our drive home. My garden was doing very well, but the raccoons had gotten a couple of chickens, while they had been running free in the field. I stopped at the Bonsons for a little chat and also to present Helen with a colorful Mexican dress for her work. When I mentioned money, I thought I

25

had stirred a wasp nest and did not pursue it any farther.

Well, my place looked different all right because Helen had cleaned everything and brought it in order as never before. My house was spotless now throughout. The Bonsons were true friends and neighbors, and I could not imagine anybody with finer ethics. What else could I only do for them?

After Helen had showed me everything, she refused to be driven home. "It's only a short walk, Arden, you still have to unpack," she said, putting me at rest.

Suddenly I remembered then and said, "By the way, you can have all the eggs for a while. I discovered that I have an allergy toward them. And with all the vegetables in the garden now, I only can each that much. If you want to come every day and get them, it sure would help me a lot. We can go over it tomorrow. Today is Thursday, I'm not going back to work 'til Monday."

Although I had my health back, the tremendous vigor I had experienced in Mexico slowly wore off again. As I was, I couldn't help but harbor some deep thoughts on the subject; was there any way to stay in that condition all the time? Had I dug into the age-old question of eternal youth? Had I touched with my rejuvenation on some ancient secret and could it be utilized today? No! With all the spiritual insight I had won, I knew already that I would do well to find my answers to the full spectrum of life away from the physical environment.

However, for the time being, most of my actions would be applied to my immediate universe. I was ready for at least a dozen projects!

Chapter 5
Cast From the Vulnerable Past

From behind several bushes on top of a little elevation right beside the approach road toward my farm gate, my eyes wandered anxiously in the direction of the Bonson place; I was expecting Willy and Hanna any moment. I hadn't seen them for over five weeks and Marg Bonson had let me know with a wise grin that the two kids had missed me a lot and our togetherness on weekends. This also would be the first time for them to stay overnight. Oh, I had so much to tell them.

When I saw Willy run up to the Bonson house and soon thereafter joined by Hanna, my excitement increased and I positioned myself so that I couldn't be detected too quickly from the road. They ran all the way and appeared out of breath when passing by into the farm yard. With cupped hands in front of my mouth, I imitated a mooing cow out of my hiding spot – I had learned to do several animal voices during the early times with my daughters -- they stopped in their tracks and looked around to investigate, so I did it again. At that moment they must have suspected me and my location because they came galloping breathlessly straight for me.

I did the cow's moo again, until we three were upon each other, laughing aloud. With arms around each other, words failed us for a while. Our hearts felt the bonds from the past, it was very evident.

With my hands on their shoulders we walked toward the house. There Hanna found her voice again and asked surprised, "How did you do the cow? I didn't know you could do that."

Grinning broadly and with raised eyebrows, as if I knew it all, my little ego got the better of me and I did several other animal voices. Needless to say, it amazed them greatly and they asked me to teach them, too.

After they had put their little bags with pajamas, toothbrushes and other overnight necessities inside the house, we walked to the garden, chicken coop and around the pond to finally reach the workshop. There I presented to each of them a colorful Mexican shirt. It was Hanna, though, who had to run quickly to the house to see herself in the mirror; it gave me an inner grin, the instinct of a woman was coming through. "Looks good?" I asked.

She nodded very satisfied. "It's so bright and different."

"That's how many of the Mexicans are dressed, men and women," I replied. Then I asked, "And what have you two been doing during my absence? I see you kept the grass neatly trimmed. How much money do I owe you, including all the odd jobs?"

Hanna answered, "We were thinking, Mister Hellmer, we always eat with you and now even stay here with you over the weekend, that ... don't pay us anymore. It evens out, you see?"

Looking at them I nodded. Then I asked, "Is that your own idea or ...?"

"Helen says, it only would be fair," Hanna informed me, but she did not sound herself.

"So Helen said that, hey?" I said. "And what do you two think? Honestly. I'm not much of a believer in second-hand interference, oldest sister or not; you are old enough to make up your own minds. What do you think, Willy?"

Hanna wanted to answer, but I raised my hand to keep her quiet. "Willy can answer for himself, Hanna, I think, please let him have his say."

But having been put on the spot, the boy seemed to be kind of uncomfortable. He raised his shoulders and searched for words; there was some awkwardness in the air, I could feel it. So I walked to the radio and tuned in my favorite classical music. Perhaps, I was too serious and made too much out of something they already had tucked away in their minds.

Looking away from them, I began to grin and said, "When I was in Mexico and met all those wonderful people in that health resort, I was thinking ... well, the beautiful feeling I had there -- in fact, we all had -- I wanted to continue it here at home then ... Naturally, I was thinking about you two guys, us three together.

28

Sure, we don't know all that well yet, but I like you a lot. I'm kind of hoping that we three can become the best of friends, that we can trust each other and tell each other everything, in spite of the big difference in age. Do you think that that is possible?"

Surprisingly, Willy was the first to answer, "I don't care about your age, Mister Hellmer, I don't care about your age and all that...'

I walked toward the boy and held out my hand with a smile. He took it, although not looking into my face. I felt his helplessness, somehow. I would try not to fail him. I said with as much warmth as I could muster and, putting my other hand onto his, "I've a suggestion to you two; how about calling me Arden from now on. I don't like to be called Mister Hellmer by friends."

"They all call you Arden at home and ... it's okay with me," Hanna burst out.

So I held out my hand to Hanna and then pulled them both closer to me so that I could put my arms around them. "I think we three will do very well."

A moment later I came back to the subject of earning money. "I do believe that you should get something for your work. Besides you should learn to handle the money you make. So here is what I shall do. Every month I'll put a small amount away for each of you and you are free to draw on it if you need some. I'm going to establish little books and boxes for the money, then you can check yourself how much you have. Right now, as I see it, you each have fourteen dollars in your accounts."

They both squeezed me with broad smiles to pass on their thanks. "Thanks a lot, Mister ... Arden," Willy expressed his gratefulness.

I asked, "Are you close to your sister, Hanna?"

"We share the same bedroom, Arden," she answered.

"She is the oldest and I'm the youngest. We are the only girls, but get along with our three brothers pretty good, I mean we never fight. Helen often helps me with school and all that. We never have any trouble with each other, if that's what you mean."

"Okay then," I said with a grin, "perhaps you can tell her, kind of, to butt out when it comes to earning a bit of money here. Do it diplomatically, though, I'm sure she means well."

Hanna laughed and said, "Mother said to her already to leave me alone with the work. She wanted me to help her clean your house."

I nodded with understanding. "So she did, did she? Well, things will even out in time, I'm sure." Then I added, "Helen sure did a wonderful job in cleaning everything around here and I'm very thankful to her. I never could have done that on my own."

A moment later I changed the subject in suggesting, "I'm not feeling like doing too much today. How about packing some lunch and a jug of juice in a rucksack and walk through the forest in the direction of the big river? We can do all the talking on our way and enjoy the wild at the same time. Let's see what animals we meet and can observe."

The two youngsters approved with enthusiasm and we three began the preparations immediately.

The children's shoes actually were not suited for an extended walk in the forest; I would have to talk about it to Hanna's mother later on.

Before leaving we tacked a note for Helen Bonson on the house door to inform her of our hike.

There were plenty of logging roads and one of them led us to an old abandoned mining town where we found plenty to explore. It seemed that all the approach roads were grown closed because nobody had been here for years. I made a mental note to get a map about this district. So far we had seen nothing but deer, too common to get excited over. As we walked from one building to another, a bear suddenly bolted out of one of the basements. It must have gotten a scent of us or heard us talk. Fifty or so yards away it stopped, turned around and raised itself on its hind legs to investigate us.

I said. "Look at the size of it. I wonder why he was in such a rush to get away from us?"

In the basement we found the carcass of a half-eaten deer. I implied, "He might have been in the process of eating or sleeping. His experience with us human beings must have been bad or he wouldn't have taken off as he did. Bears are very protective of their food. They have one of the finest smelling organs, by the way, on top of the list of all wild animals. I once read that they can smell out mushrooms a couple of hundred yards away without having the wind in their favor."

We three did not have one dull moment. Nature was just the thing to bond us closer together.

* * *

Back home again and after supper, we watched a science program on TV. To my surprise they demonstrated on this show, in a minute way -- something I had experienced in one of my former dreams a few months before -- that one can move and influence things and events with his thoughts. What a lucky break, or was it an invisible hand again, trying to open a door to my inventive desire and ability? This was exactly what I had planned for my next project; namely I wanted to build little receiver-relays, something I would be able to actuate with my concentrated mind power. Those little ... gadgets – I didn't know yet what to call them – would in turn activate anything electric I wanted to switch on or off from a distance.

Through my dream I knew already how it worked, and in building one of these gadgets now, I wanted to prove to myself how well it worked in our physical environment, and also, how well I would be able to concentrate my mind.

Anyway, the kids and I were very excited about this project, not that I let on about the dream I had had. Until bedtime we three made drawing after drawing, how best to implement these little devices of the future.

* * *

When I was standing in the darkness of a house and watched a scene playing in front of me, as if it was one of those obscene movies, I suddenly realized that I was in my dream state. I wished that I could have turned it off, but was not able to, as if I was made to observe this play. Only to me it wasn't play, it was real.

The two actors were a man and a little boy, they could have been father and son. In the dimness of the room I had no difficulties making out the detailed going-ons, as the man forced the boy to cater to his sexual wishes. In between I could hear the boy's cries; he clearly revolted against his oppressor's wishes.

At one time the youngster was able to wiggle himself away from the man and I heard him cry out: "No! No! I don't want to!" To my utter amazement and agony I recognized him to be Willy.

The cries of the boy sounded so real, so lifelike, that it pulled me out of the dream into the waking state, yet I still was able to hear the anguished wails of the boy. Sitting up in bed and rubbing my eyes, I tried to get my bearings. What was going on? I was wide awake now and not in my dream experience anymore.

Then it came to me in a sudden awareness; I heard Willy's agonizing cries in his bedroom; he must have had the very same dream. As I rushed out of my room, I almost bumped into Hanna outside Willy's bedroom door.

Upon entering his room, the boy was in an awful state, still calling out: "No! No! I don't want to!"

Quickly then I took him into my arms and said with a soothing voice, "Willy, Willy, it's me, Arden. Wake up, you are safe now; it's me, Arden." His tight arms around my neck were an indication that he was awake now and aware of his waking state; he recognized me as his true friend he could trust.

A flood of tears followed, what most of us would call a nightmare. However, I knew better. I was there, too. I said to Hanna, "He had a bad dream; you can go to bed again, I'll stay with him for a while." I could see the concern on Hanna's face, but she was satisfied with what I had assured her and left for her own bedroom.

'I wonder who that man was?' I thought. 'I hope he is not one of his mother's friends, visiting her frequently. I better speak with Marg and Bill and see whether we should contact a district social worker.'

Willy's grip had loosened and he sank back onto his pillow. I was astonished over the question leaving my mouth then. "Who was that man, Willy?"

Without wondering how I knew, he answered with detached emotions, as if he had had enough of painful experiences. "That's my father." Then, a moment later. "Before mom divorced him. I only was a little boy then." He kind of uttered the sentences as if not himself.

I was glad to hear that. At least, this man was out of his life now on the physical level. 'That boy needs a father,' I thought, 'and it looks that I'm going to be the one; a father figure. Destiny has brought us together again, I can see that. The way he trusts me. The bands of our past lives' bonds come through as if we had known and lived together only recently.'

Willy's voice brought me back to the present. "I'm okay now, Arden," he breathed deeply.

"I'm still wide awake, Willy," I tried to make him feel at ease, "if you want to tell me the whole story? You see, I, too, was there in my dream, I saw it all happen."

32

He put his hands behind his head and whispered, as if afraid that somebody might hear him. "Dad was always drunk when he came into my bedroom. But mom knew about it and never helped. I guess she was more afraid than I was. She is okay today, as long as she doesn't marry one of those guys she's ..."

'Oh, I'm so glad he trusts me,' my thoughts followed his confession, "I'm glad," I said out loud, "now, at least I know what's going on and can help. Yeah, I understand, Willy." Then I had an idea and said, "If you are ever pestered again like that -- often people are not themselves when they are drunk -- you come to me and stay here for a while. Okay?"

He nodded and had a quick glance at me to make sure that I meant what I had said. I, too, had whispered my sentences and said now slowly with the same quiet but assured voice, "You can trust me, Willy." And I took his hand. With his head turned away, he took my hand on his cheek where his tears wet my fingers. It was the yearning for love.

I had the feeling that he would have liked to put his arms around my neck and hear the words out of my mouth, "I love you, Son!" Tears of reinforcement rolled down my cheeks.

* * *

None of us three were late sleepers, but this morning we were particularly early and prepared breakfast at six. No doubt Willy's terrible dream experience had something to do with it. As my mind lingered on it, I thought, 'Perhaps we should spend the day with something to give the children more insight into the unknown; behind the scenes of dreams, so to speak. It sure would help the boy in his plight. He probably had them before and is bound to have some more of this nature. Or was the dream designed for us both, to open an important avenue, a happening of the future? I aimed to find out. And as long as this whole 'thing' was still warm, we might as well probe into the subject now.' My thoughts went along those lines.

We were quietly eating, when Hanna brought up the subject of flying saucers. "When you were gone, Arden, we read some of your books, as you suggested we do. You think that the people from the space ships are real? I mean, they don't act like us and the things they can do. We don't understand it."

I was grateful to her to have brought it up. That subject somehow was related to dreams also, namely, it, too, came from beyond the physical realm, the Astral worlds. But, I had to be very careful, after all I didn't want to interfere with their religious beliefs and bring their parents down on my back. Perhaps it would be wise to speak with the Bonsons first and find out where they stood on this matter.

I nodded with an elated smile. "I know precisely what you mean. When I started reading about this, shortly after I came to the coast, I was as puzzled as you are now, but I didn't give up, I read many other books and magazines." Then I continued, "I tell you what we'll do, perhaps we should make this a day of ... probing explorations into the unknown." I grinned with raised eyebrows and a pointed index finger toward the ceiling. "We can do some more reading, out loud I mean, and then discuss it with a lot of questions and answers to follow. Something like a natural and spontaneous instruction class, where all of us are the students and teachers at the same time. Free spirited kind of, in the manner we discussed those gadgets last night. I'm not all that knowledgeable, you know. Well, what do you say?"

I could see the satisfied grins on the children's faces, they obviously liked the idea. It was the new concept of teacher-student relationship which intrigued them most, something I found out later.

So quickly our relationship would become a bond of equality and it never was broken or abused in all the years hence. At one time I had hoped to attain this friendly give-and-take accord between juvenile and adult with my daughters, but failed, unfortunately; it mostly was out of immaturity on my part.

Hanna's question ripped me out of my thoughts: "Can we discuss everything? I mean really everything? What I mean is ... well, you are an adult and we're only eleven and a half years old."

"First of all, I'm not your parent," I answered with a smile. "I cannot deceive your parents in discussing a subject which they don't want us to discuss, and I have to be the judge of that. The trust we three have in each other also exists between your parents and me. In time we'll find out where our common ground lies and where not. You surely understand that?

"Secondly, there are also subjects your inexperienced minds are not ready for as yet and you have to be conditioned slowly; something you also understand, I'm, sure. You may believe, however, that there is nothing under the sun which I will not try to prepare you for, if I can help it. If I know it, you will hear it from me, I guarantee it. If I don't know it, we will buy books, read them and discuss the subjects afterward, okay?"

After I had finished the last sentence I kind of wondered whether I had gone too far, but felt amazingly comfortable with what I had suggested to them.

After breakfast we first went to the chickens to feed them and then walked around the pond and eventually wound up in the little boat, which I rowed on and off, as our discussions permitted.

The obvious first questions I had to answer were about flying saucers; are they real? Where do they come from? Why do only a few of us see them? Although only a dozen or so books on the subject could be found in my little library, I fortunately had a bit more insight about UFOs and related topics through my dreams.

I began by telling them about the Astral worlds first. I had to be very careful, though, because I did not yet know where their parents stood in their beliefs and what I was allowed to reveal to my young friends. I said, "There are other worlds out there," I pointed to the sky, "and they have different dimensions. We here on Earth, in our physical universe, have only three dimensions; the things we observe through geometry with our physical eyes. However, as we increase our awareness of dimensions to the fourth, the fifth and above, we add concepts not visible and certainly not known to most of us, with the exception of some nosey, seeking and adventuresome people who read a lot of unorthodox books to enlarge on their knowledge.

"Some say that the Bible is full of four dimensional experiences, but that most of us interpret it with our three-dimensional understanding. That's why there are so many disagreements to the point of fighting to the death even. Well, I'm not a student of the Bible, I only can pass on what I've read over the years."

A moment later and having rowed a couple of times, I continued, "But I know that there is a world where they live with four dimensions, where, to give you only one example, their thoughts are able to move things, including themselves. As we move here from one place to another with our legs and other mechanical means, there they use their thoughts to do the very same. That's only one aspect, though, there are others.

"The vibrations in those words are finer than ours and that's why most of us can't see those beings and the material they use, like the flying saucers. Some of us, however, are born with, or

35

develop, this ability in turning up our vibratory rate and then can see into the fourth dimension and the flying saucers. So, there might be two people standing right beside each other, but only one of them sees the UFO. Can you see now why it's so controversial? No two people talk alike over the very same subject. It is my experience to best stay away from any heated discussions. If one knows the whole spectrum of the fourth dimension, there is not much to argue about the rights or wrongs because one is sure, no need to rub it in.

"We three will keep on studying and discussing all this in our small circle and let others do the arguing of something they don't know too much about to begin with."

"But some look so real in the book you have," Willy said with a face of doubt. "If they are in their fourth dimension, I mean, how could they take those pictures?"

"That's an excellent point, Willy," I answered, surprised. "In the beginning, I wondered about that myself, too. I asked myself, are they using a special camera or a special film? No they didn't. I kept on wondering until I read that those intelligent beings can lower their vibratory rate to ours here on Earth and then become visible to us and also show up on pictures. But there are other flying saucers that come from planets where they are still in their third dimension as we are. Naturally, we can see them with our physical eyes and use our ordinary cameras on them for pictures.

"I suspect that there are many people on other planets, out in the heavens, technically much more advanced to what we know and power their space vehicles with the cosmic energy. They are able to cover to us unimaginable long distances in a relatively short time. I don't believe that they are from our own solar system because none of our planets can sustain physical life, as you probably already know."

"What's the cosmic power?" Willy asked.

"Boy, now you really got me," I answered, laughing and raising my shoulders and eyebrows. "But I can tell you this much; there is energy everywhere, whether here or in the vastness of space. Some advanced beings have simply learned to tap it and use it to fly their space vehicles. It's an invisible and boundless fuel, there for the taking."

"We could invent it, Arden!" Hanna called out very seriously.

I simply chuckled, perhaps more to myself, and answered with far away thoughts, "Wouldn't that be something! We fly into space and then ..." shaking my head, I said a bit later, "no, it would be too far out. There are many other things we can invent right now to be used in our immediate environment and we shall concentrate on that."

For a long time our thoughts went on their own individual trips, until I aired my thoughts on the subject of dreams. "By the way, did you know that our dreams are often also happening in the fourth dimension of the Astral world?" I quickly glanced at Willy, whether my cutting into this subject had any effect on him. But he seemed detached enough. I went on, "Many of us go into those worlds where people live in the fourth dimension. I wish I could tell you more about those planes, but I'm a novice almost as much as you are.

"I know a bit more about dreams, though, and record them all in a journal during the night, shortly after I wake up and have had them. Fully awake in the morning, I try to interpret them. The meaning of most dreams is not the way one experiences them; they come scrambled kind of, so one has to learn to unscramble and translate them and use the real meaning for his benefit. I have two books on the subject; however, after reading them, I'm not much smarter and closer in translating my dreams. I believe that one has to establish his own code eventually. The only way to do that properly is to start a journal and record all the dreams."

"I want to start a dream book, too, Arden," Hanna called out, determined. "I dream so often and we can discuss them here then, couldn't we?"

I nodded.

"Me, too, Arden," Willy fell in, equally sure. "After that last night." He raised his shoulders and his face showed disgust, but I also detected fear.

I tried to add some more thoughts on the subject, of what I understood about it. "At times past happenings are recorded in our subconsciousness and will then come out in our dreams because they are so painful at the time and because our mind was not able to handle the situation in a detached way. Our involved emotions made those subconscious imprints so powerful and that's why they stay implanted.

"I wish I could give you a complete discourse, but my knowledge so far is pretty limited. I don't know too much more than you do.

37

"One of the doctors in the Mexican resort was telling us that if we can learn to keep our feelings and emotions out of our present and future daily happenings, we never will be pestered again by anguish or emotional pain and are happy for the rest of our lives without ever any kind of sickness. Can you believe that? In any case, I'll order some books he recommended and we'll see from there on. There are about a hundred or so books about all the different discussions we had there, and in time I want to write for them all. So you can see that a lot of knowledge and wisdom was given out at that place and we have to wait and see what goodness will materialize out of all that reading eventually.

"By the way, I almost forgot one of the most important aspects," I went on. "In many of my dreams I'm assisted and guided by a dream master or masters. I never saw any of them, but just the same they speak to me. It's not in actual words, although one might get the impression in the beginning. They are high spiritual beings with vast god powers, something like Christ had in his time. If you are ever pestered again, Willy, call on a master. I'm quite sure that one of them will help. Just call out: "Master, help me, please!" Do it several times. He'll come, I'm certain.

"You see, I was there, too," I went on, "and saw it all, as I was telling you already. I think that my dream master took me there to observe it, so that later on I knew what actually happened. I'm so thankful that he did because now I understand and can help you in some way."

As the day began to warm and the sun appeared on and off from behind the clouds, we three spread out a blanket in the grass near the house and continued a lazy conversation on related subjects.

When our minds and discussions eventually returned to the thought operating gadgets we intended to build, we decided that they would get our whole attention later on after lunch in the workshop. In a way, I was glad; our consciousness in the morning had been too heavy, we needed something more enjoyable for our minds.

Chapter 6
It Happened a Century Ago

When I came to this continent I had had this deep-down fleeting feeling in my guts, and it still stirred me now and then in moments of reflection, but it did particularly when I watched a western movie on TV with Indians on the attack. It could excite me terribly and at times left me awake for half the night afterward. In fact, it had become so bad that I stopped watching this kind of a show.

However, of what I knew about reincarnation through some of my dreams, and also of what I had read in a dozen or so books on the subject, it made me wonder whether this unusually strong feeling had any past life connection. The thing was, though, that I was unable to turn it off, no matter how hard I tried; there always seemed to be a second me in the deep crevices of my consciousness, which I was not able to deal with and control.

* * *

Right from the beginning I was aware that I had had a dream experience; my dream master had let me know and he was the one who had initiated the dream to begin with, in drawing the past into the present by this medium; or, as it were, he had taken me back on the time track.

Most of the time, I was not aware of the dream process until much later when in the waking state again.

In the beginning of this dream I saw a family around the Sunday morning breakfast table. It was in the house of a country-town doctor in Germany around the middle of the nineteenth century. The father was speaking to his son, Hermann, the second youngest boy of the five children. Suddenly I realized that I was that boy, who had just graduated from high school.

"Berlin is a big city," I heard my father say, "where young boys are often tempted by vices. I trust you to stay away from them."

I was prepared by my father to go to the Berlin university to become a doctor also. Naturally, as one of the sons, I would follow in the footsteps of my dad who was a successful country physician in this mid-western German town.

Everything was packed already and on Monday it would be goodbye for almost a year. Being still from the old-fashioned school, my father had hired an experienced driver with his horses and wagon who was well familiar with the route to the capital city. He did not trust the railroad, which was not that well established at the time.

The day had come and my mother and sisters had lost a lot of tears. When the driver came from the kitchen with a basket full of food and drink for our journey and took his seat, we were on our way. I didn't feel all that good either in my stomach.

After a half a day's drive, I joined the coachman on his seat up front in the carriage. Although I was exposed to the fresh wind and rain at times, I did not feel so lonely there and enjoyed the shouts of the horseman, rushing on his team of horses.

Most of the inns in those days were located at road crossings and often the owner had a grain mill at the same time. At these lodgings, good food for man and animal was available besides a comfortable overnight's stay, but the horses could also be changed for a fresh team.

In the afternoon on the second day, Berlin came into sight. I never had seen so many people and so many rows of big houses. And all the different horse transportations; my eyes and mind had an awful lot to see and to digest.

We stopped in front of a three-story building; it would be my room and board for the next few years. This place was only a short distance from the university and well known with a good reputation. Mother Reinke, a widow, came waddling out of the house to greet me. If her corpulent body was an indication of good food, I had nothing to worry about.

My hostess took me around the ground floor, where the dining and living rooms were located and we wound up in the kitchen, where she offered me a piece of delicious cake. She said, "You must be happy here, young man; every time you need something, come to Mother Reinke, I will do my best to please you."

A girl took me to the third floor, where my room was located. She pointed the meal and bathing times out to me and gave me a weekly schedule. She said, "If you need water, pull this string on the wall and one of us girls will bring it to you immediately."

Well, everything worked out smoothly and I lost some of my home-sickness, after I had met all the other students, most of them around my age.

At the university it didn't take the well-established students long to introduce me to all their negative customs, namely the evening and weekend parties of beer drinking and loud singing. Here the older students dared us younger ones to all kinds of mischief and I was no exception, not heeding my father's warnings. With the little pranks, the law often looked the other way, knowing that we would bring things in order again and pay for the damages. But, as naive as I was, I let myself push and dare to even greater pranks. As a newcomer, I felt proud to have been chosen.

My expulsion from the university came rather quickly and dramatically, when I was caught, as there had been several witnesses, pulling a safety pin out of a public horse-carriage wheel axle. After the wheel had come off, not only did the horses begin to run wild and drag the three-wheeled vehicle with screaming occupants through the streets, but the loose wheel rolled over nearby playing children, hurting two of them badly.

After the court session and having been sentenced to six months in prison, the university dean and his colleagues were not far behind in their decision. There was nothing anybody could have done; I was condemned to not only be a prisoner, but also having failed particularly my father. The future and my pride were destroyed through this unfortunate happening, and it was utterly impossible to think in terms of a happy home life again.

In my prison cell I had enough time to do a lot of sensible thinking. I decided that the least thing I could do for my parents, siblings and their good reputation was to leave them for good. I had decided to go to America and begin a new life. I already had caused enough sleepless nights for them back home, now I was determined not to be of any more burden.

When the answer about my decision came back from my father and his reluctant agreement, I was glad. In those days in

Germany (and still today, occasionally) a reputation of a well-to-do family was a very important part of society. A 'black sheep' who could tarnish the name often was sent off to the 'New World', where there was no worry about somebody's past.

A half year later in Hamburg, I was about to board a steam liner to America. My parents, brothers, and sisters hugged me again and again and even dad shed a few tears.

On the high seas I tried to concentrate on my future, what was I heading for? What was in store for me? Father had given me a few hundred dollars, I had a good education and was healthy. What else could I ask for.

America! In spite of the rain, we all stood outside, full of excitement. After docking, families and friends were waiting ashore to greet the newcomers, and for a moment my emotions buckled up.

Quickly I went past the authorities with my baggage. After I had stored my belongings, with the exception of a small bag, my first thoughts went to finding a job in the huge city of New York.

Upon arrival I walked the streets and met another German, who had been there for four weeks already. He almost cried on my shoulder, trying to tell me that he was not able to find work. Quickly I realized that we two together would only be a handicap to each other and I got rid of him. When I saw a sign at the hotel entrance shortly after this painful encounter, indicating they were looking for kitchen help, I entered and soon faced the manager in his office.

He said in German, "You just arrived from Germany and want a job."

"How do you know that?" I stuttered, astounded.

"One can see it," he grinned. "Your clothes, your looks. And how is your English?" And he changed into the English language. "What do you know about the hotel business? Nothing, I can see that."

"I'm eager to learn. I can understand you, but still have difficulties to speak it," I replied.

"Well, you can have the job in the kitchen," he said. "You probably have a better education."

"My father is a medical doctor." I tried to impress him, but he didn't let me finish the sentence.

42

"This is America, forget about the Old Country," he informed me. "Here, you start new. Nobody cares about what you were and about your family."

He sounded harsh, but I liked him. Then he introduced me to the head cook in the kitchen, who was French. He would be my boss for the next few weeks. My bedroom was in the attic, where I was crammed together with three others.

The other helpers in the kitchen were French, Polish, Italian and Belgian. The chef would scold them all the time when they did not speak English, which actually came easy to me. I had to do everything, but mostly I washed dishes.

In four weeks the manager called me to his office again and said, "Your English has improved enough, you do well not to listen to the others. I shall give you a job in the hotel lobby to help the new guests with the baggage. In this hotel there is plenty of room for good workers, with better pay, of course."

After three more months I began to ask myself, whether this hotel work was really for me. There was a deep down yearning within me, longing for action, much more action than I had here.

When two young men checked in one day, I had a long talk with them in their room. They owned a gold mine and were in town to buy more equipment. In their first big 'scoop', as they called it, they already had made twenty thousand dollars.

Excitedly, I asked them whether they could use another partner with some funds, meaning me, of course.

Naturally, they were very reluctant at first; however, the next morning they told me that I was welcome to join them because I looked honest and was physically strong.

After a year and a half in my new country and learning fast the underground mining trade, my yearning came through again. I had become good on horseback, pretty good in fighting off Indians and shady characters. I had increased my capital considerably, although we had not struck the expected rich gold vein.

My two partners paid me out, but only let me go reluctantly because, in having become a crack-shot, I was very valuable to them. We three had made an excellent team, where trust was written in capital letters, we had become good friends.

I bought myself a good horse with all the equipment and food one needed in the wild on his own. For days I rode, not seeing a soul and living off the country. I felt elated and good, until I came upon a burnt-out wagon and three dead people, one of them a woman. I buried the bodies while keeping a wary eye on the surroundings for would-be attackers. This incident upset me terribly; it was the other side of wild America and my horse and I were facing it all by ourselves.

Eventually, I came to the Ohio River and the first big town since I had left my friends at the mine. The saloons and hotels were full of people all talking about California and gold discovered there. I heard the craziest stories and was sure that not even half of them came close to the truth, but I got the gold fever, too. I had my first experience with one of the easy girls, but kicked her out of the hotel room after I saw her going through my pockets for easy cash. I had to laugh about it later in the morning because I had some gold hidden away in the saddle bags and the money around my neck in a little leather bag.

In the next town I ran into a well-organized wagon train and asked their leader whether I could join them. They all looked like mature and sensible people, old hands in the wilds. In those days it was much easier to size somebody up, and by judging my good horse and equipment, they decided that I was their kind and added me to their group of five women and eleven men. I was detailed to the last wagon, that of a middle-aged couple.

Early in the morning we were on our way. Henry, our leader, had been to the west coast before and he knew the route. At the mighty Mississippi River we crossed the water by ferry. Now the country became even more wild and we all had our eyes open for any unusual movements -- this was strictly Indian territory where no white people had settled down as yet.

The first night was quiet, but next morning we saw smoke signals in the distance. Henry lost no time in reminding us again that the redskins had detected us and surely would trail us from now on. In the late afternoon we found a good spot for the night and made camp. Except for the calls of some night birds, probably the Indians conversing with each other, nothing happened.

We hardly were on our way again next morning when we heard, faintly at first, then pounding louder and louder, what sounded like a thousand drums. Suddenly we heard Henry's yell: "Buffalo stampede! Take cover! Quick! Quick!" Fortunately, there was a hill straight ahead, and the wagons who didn't make it on top, raced behind it in its shadow for protection. It wasn't a minute too early. The buffalo herd parted around each side of the mound and left us unharmed in their wake, wrapped in a thick cloud of dust.

When we finally formed our wagon train again, Henry said with a hard grin, "That was close! The redskins looked for easy picking. Most likely they are only a small band and don't feel strong enough for a frontal attack. We better stay in the open as much as possible. Keep close together."

Again we found a favorable place in the late afternoon to make camp. Nothing happened until a couple or so hours after midnight, when one of our guards fired a shot, and another, and another. Then the famous screams of a dozen Indians reached our ears, but we were ready. Their arrows didn't do us much harm.

Only one shot was fired at us by our attackers and the bullet hit me in the heart. Instantly, I was out of my body, to watch a bit later some of the men and women assembled around my corpse. Their faces indicated that I was dead, all right.

Then I heard from my dream master and guide by impression, "You didn't last long in that incarnation, but those past imprints surface today and give you this deep-down and low feeling you are so uncomfortable with at times." That's all he said.

Immediately, I woke up and laid awake until dawn.

* * *

I had no difficulties writing every phase and detail of this dream down. It made me shudder that I should have died so quickly with a shot to the heart, only one shot fired by the Indians. And thoughts worked themselves into my mind, what would I have done then with a life to a ripe old age? And what of my parents and siblings? Did they ever hear of my death?

At breakfast I became aware of a noise in my left ear. It sounded like a high-pitched turbine in the background. It was very steady and did not even cease at work nor during the next two days. Not that it was uncomfortable, but I began to wonder whether the dream was its originator. It certainly wasn't natural.

Before I made too much of the matter, or even might have gone to a physician, my dream master approached me on the third night in the dream state again and said, "You are hearing Spirit, the voice of God. Be elated because It will help you to get over the past; It will help you to get over those bothersome old roots. Receive It with love."

Then I saw the master's face for the first time and his love

45

came forth and penetrated my heart and every fiber of my being.

He looked like a man in his late thirties, bald headed and clean-shaven. Oh, I was so grateful to finally have seen one of them, Yes, compassion and humility come to mind, that's what he omitted mostly. Now I knew the real meaning of love.

Coming home from work next day, Marg Bonson stopped me at their place and we had a quick chat through the car window. She said, "Hanna asked us for the Bible after she came back from you. We're not church people and wondered."

"Ha, ha," I laughed, "she did, hey?" I put her mind to rest in saying, "Don't worry, Marg, I'm not trying to make true believers out of the kids. I myself hardly read the Bible and wouldn't call myself a Christian. We discussed the fourth dimension and I was telling them that there are several references to it in the Bible, something I read once."

Marg laughed and said, "I told Bill already that you didn't look like a religionist to me. Actually, we don't mind you know, as long as you don't make a big thing out of it and keep it in its place."

I answered, "Science is on our minds, Marg, not religion. We discuss everything under the sun, including ticklish subjects, but not in a fanatic way. Can you believe it, we even talked about flying saucers and in that connection came to the fourth dimension. I've several books about it and they read some of them during my absence. Nothing hurtful in them."

"We trust you, Arden," Marg patted me on the arm. "We ourselves believe to never hide anything from the children. But, as farmers, as busy as we are most of the times, we might have neglected the kids perhaps in not discussing with them what you've touched now."

"I tell you what," I tried to close the subject, "if I come across something I'm not sure of, I'm going to speak with you first, okay?"

On the last stretch home, I talked to myself. "Nice people, nice to have as neighbors. I hardly know them and already we trust each other like old friends. Maybe there is a past life connection, too. It sure wouldn't surprise me."

Chapter 7
Mind Tinkers

Hanna, Willy and I were intensely busy in my workshop trying to put together our first prototype of a remote control gadget, which we then intended to operate with our concentrated mind power. A certain generated thought would be the medium to switch on or off the electrical appliance we contemplated to operate. For the time being it only would be a light bulb. With other words, the process would go from mind-thought to receiver to relay to light bulb.

I was soldering the receiver together and hooking up the relay while the children tried to fasten a light socket to a board under my direction. Last we put up a little receiver antenna.

I couldn't afford to be excited or distracted, so I motioned to them to be very quiet to give me a good chance for my first try. Was the receiver sensitive enough to be activated by my concentrated mind power? Closing my eyes, I sat in silence in my easy chair and tried to excite a certain frequency with a thought pattern as I had been shown in the dream. It worked! I tried it again and sure enough the relay clicked, all three of us had heard it. We were elated, that it should be that easy. Of course, this was only a short distance and one had to see later on how far away one could operate this gadget.

Suddenly I called out with a joyous grin: "We'll call them mind tinkers, that's an appropriate name."

"What does tinkers mean, Arden?" Hanna asked.

I pointed to a dictionary we always had around and they both leafed through it. "You think they only be tinkers to us?" she asked.

I raised my eyebrows in a wait-and-see manner and answered, "It all essentially depends on us. Time and experience will tell us their importance and the priority we are willing to give them."

I don't think they understood the meaning of my answer, but they didn't follow it up, so I kept quiet, too, for the time being.

Finally we had hooked it all up and hung it on the wall near the big door with the light bulb plugged into the electrical outlet.

One surely could have heard a needle drop on the dirt floor; visibly nothing was in motion, though. When the light on the wall went off, we knew that my mind current had been strong enough and had reached the tinker. We were so excited over the success that we put our arms around each other, now that we could let our emotions go.

Next, naturally the youngsters wanted to give it a try also, but their young minds had their difficulties, no matter how much I tried to explain it. "Remember, the attunement to this particular frequency is the most important thing," and I pointed to the chart again I had made for them.

I was at a loss on how best I could explain to these two inexperienced minds, who never had meditated nor contemplated before, how to focus their thoughts on something I couldn't even put into words. I had been shown in a dream. The fourth dimension! It came to me.

"Remember the third and fourth dimensions?" I called out. "This is something similar. Our mind power is invisible and we are trying to use it on something visible. Two different dimensions are involved, which makes it so hard to explain and understand."

Finally, while sitting at lunch, an idea from the Mexican resort came to mind. There we had examined the different thought bands and how to tune our minds into them. But the children were too intense and still couldn't do it. So I suggested to forget it for the rest of the afternoon; they had reached a point where they couldn't relax anymore, a very essential quality.

Well, it took them another three weeks until they finally were able to operate the mind tinkers, and I sure was glad that it was over. This whole affair had become too unnatural, too intense, too everything, and I was not able to turn it off again. It clearly made me aware of our difference in ages, while I could handle it with my seasoned mind, they could not. It taught me a great deal, something to remember for our future relationship.

In the meantime, we had built half a dozen of them and I had become really good in operating them, even from a distance of five miles. We had a MT (mind tinker) hooked up to the kitchen stove, one to the chicken food dispenser and all kinds of things which would give us experience and a lot of laughs, like the car signal lights, for instance.

I was looking for an independent future, where I was able to live off my inventions eventually, something like an early retirement. However, when it came to the MTs, I had decided that they never should be commercialized; I had no intention selling them. They soon would be misused by greedy people who couldn't care less about good ethics.

At the moment we were trying to put an MT into the steering column lock of the car; I thought it to be a good mind training. While driving and at the same time keeping the steering unlocked with controlled and concentrated thoughts, one would become perfected at the game and put his mind into top shape.

For our car runs we used the unkept fields of my farm and the short road to the Bonson place. So there was no danger of an accident at all, we only might get off our driving path and have a good laugh about it. We had installed a switch in the car trunk where the MT could be turned on or off. The Bonsons knew about our project and didn't mind the children driving. Besides we always were riding abreast on the front seat.

During all this time I had to wonder about my young friends, about their technical understanding; after all, they were hardly twelve years old. I couldn't have asked for better assistants, and, often enough, took their advice in solving a problem.

After a couple of weekends of driving around and back and forth, the Bonson adults really began to wonder what our mind and thought enterprise was all about and, to my surprise, they aired their desire to know more about it. So I gave them a book to read first and promised to follow it up with a talk.

When we three adults finally were sitting together then and I explains to them what we had been doing on weekends in running the car as often as we did, they were utterly amazed that their daughter was able to do that. I said, "Do you understand the training I'm trying to give the two children, and myself also, of course? It'll help them in school and for the rest of their lives, too. Our uncontrolled emotions are often interfering with the concentration of thoughts, and not many of us have the discipline to reverse that. In any case, there are so many benefits coming with this exercise, I noticed it on myself already."

"Can we try it?" asked Bill.

"Sure," I answered. "I brought a MT with a light along for you." I went outside to the car to get it.

But they couldn't do it and my demonstration didn't make it any easier either.

Then Marg said, "I'd like to see Hanna doing it. I think we have a very smart girl."

We were sitting in the kitchen, so they called their daughter in from the living room. "Would you do that for us, Hanna, please." Marg pointed to the MT with the light bulb.

"Sure, Mom." She sat down and had the light turned off in ten seconds. She did that several times.

It obviously dumbfounded the parents because words failed them for a few minutes. That their daughter was able to do that!

When Bill began to shake his head, I said, "that's discipline for you, Bill."

After Hanna had joined her siblings again in the next room, Bill said, "That only can be of benefit. I want to learn that, too. Can we keep this thing?"

"Sure," I said, "you can have more of them. You should see all the things we run with our thoughts by remote control."

Suddenly Marg laughed out, "Then we can run our whole farm from inside the house."

I had to laugh about her comment and Bill chuckled and said, "Wouldn't that be something."

"I'm very thankful to you, Arden," Bill said. "Our daughter has changed much for the better since visiting you on weekends."

"I would appreciate if this doesn't get out," I said. "If the business world ever gets wind of this invention, you know darn well what'll happen with it. Please ask your other children also to keep it to themselves."

Bill Bonson nodded in thought, then answered, "You have a good point there, Arden. Yeah, we must keep it among us, that's for sure."

"Don't worry, Arden, it's safe with us," Marg gave her husband support and assurance to me.

50

* * *

When I woke up I was instantly wide awake, remembering a dream. It had been very revealing in that the adult Bonsons had been there, too.

It must have been in England around the Middle Ages. We all had spoken English and the location indicated a castle. While we three conversed, I had a glance out of one of the windows, overlooking the castle courtyard and saw several knights in a sporty battle with their swords and shields.

By what we three had talked about, Bill Bonson and I must have been brothers and the masters of the castle while Marg Bonson was our sister.

This experience back in time didn't take very long, but it sure put some light on the fact that we three knew each other from way back and the inner recognition was still there.

The last words or impression I remember came from my dream master: "Almost everybody in your world is related with each other and it goes back thousands of years and many lifetimes. It's not an accident that most of you are your own ancestors, it stands to reason."

That thought almost took the wits out of me. Could that really be?

The Bonsons and I related ... how often had we been together?

Many other questions milled through my head while I wrote down the dream. This certainly was my lifetime of revelations.

Chapter 8
The Devil's Field of Ploy

Two and a half years had passed by and spring was just about to make its entrance again. Many important experiences and happenings had traversed our lives.

The children had taken a vast interest in building model gliders. In the beginning I had taught them the fundamentals, but from there on they took to it -- with only a little guidance from me here and there -- like young artists longing for their talent's outlet. They simply loved it and showed a lot of creativity. There also was some breakage, but we had much fun and created beautiful flying models (reminding me of a happy boyhood). However, when the children's workshop teacher tried to put some bitterness upon their model-flying venture, Bill Bonson and I 'stepped in', so to speak.

Well, it happened this way: Willy and Hanna had taken their best flying model to school to demonstrate their latest creation; and it not only astounded their fellow students, but also the teacher. Unfortunately, his reaction was negative and he told them very bluntly that he didn't think they could've built it themselves. He discredited them before the whole class.

When Marg Bonson phoned me that Hanna had come home almost crying, I decided to see her teacher and give him a piece of my mind. Mentioning this to her, she told me that Bill had aired the very same desire. So we both went.

When we two were alone with the teacher, I could clearly see and hear that anger was mixed into Bill's words when he said, "Mister Hollow, I'm here to complain about the way you made a fool of my daughter in front of her classmates. You had no right nor reason to do that. I want you to apologize to Hanna and to Willy also, because they both worked on the model together very diligently without anybody's help. I want you to do that in front of their class where you had discredited them with your words. They were deeply hurt."

The teacher's face had become dark red with embarrassment – laced with some anger, too, I thought – but before any words came over his lips, I said, "You see, Mister Hollow, I'm a neighbor of the Bonson family and the two children are with me on weekends where they build their models in my large workshop. Of course, I showed and helped them in the beginning, having had some experience as a boy and during my time in the German Air Force during the war. I can assure you, though, that the model they brought here to school was done entirely on their own. The children used some of my material and the tools and that's all. Hanna and Willy designed and built the model without my helping hands, I can assure you of that."

After a short thought I continued. "You see I'm an inventor and there is a saying between us three: 'If you don't know it, chew it over first and then swallow it.' It's meant symbolically, of course. The meaning of it is that individually we are on our own and should not depend on others for help; at least, we should give it a good try first. I never cater to the children with any petty stuff, because the Bonsons and I believe in the early self-efficiency of children. Besides, I haven't got the time to help them with any details."

It was very clear by now that the teacher wished he could vanish under the floorboards. He finally stuttered: "I'm very sorry ... I'm sorry for what I said to the children and I will apologize to them."

Bill stood up and said very matter of factly: "Before the class, Mister Hollow."

I had gotten up, too, and followed my neighbor our of the room; suddenly he seemed to be in a hurry, as if to avoid an argument with the teacher, who had not the slightest intention of doing so, I was quite sure.

Outside, he just nodded to me with a grin, as if to say, 'We gave it to him, didn't we?'

While entering my car for work, I said, "See you tonight, Bill."

I guess my neighbor didn't feel all that comfortable, realizing, perhaps, that anger had gotten the better of him, something he hadn't intended doing. Not that I felt all that pleased, we kind of had ganged up on the poor teacher, who hadn't even got in a single word for his defense. We two drove off in our individual vehicles without any farther comment.

Having sold my second major invention with a good financial return, I was heading for the last week of work at the aircraft company. From now on I was free insofar that I was not depending on anybody else for my upkeep anymore. Only three years before, I never would've dreamed that I could've accomplished this feat so quickly. But everything fell into place as if an invisible hand had led me on in this endeavour.

When I saw the children the next weekend, they had run all the way from the Bonson place to tell me the news about their teacher. He had apologized to t hem and quit the school. Hanna called out, still half out of breath: "Since Wednesday, we have Mister Hopkins and he thinks we did an excellent job with the airplane. We're going to fly it again next week with better weather."

I did some deep nodding, happy to hear the news, and also some deep thinking. There probably had been a lot of action behind the scenes at their school. Was it the invisible hand again?

"Are you really at home now all the time, Arden?" Willy asked.

"Yessir," was my answer with a wise grin, "and already I've laid out a new project; its going to be a dandy one." After the two had taken a seat I explained. "As you know I did some glider flying during the war in the German Air Force. Anyway, since then I never stopped dreaming of wanting to fly with my own human power; meaning, I want to stay up in the air, using my own muscle power. I already have some good ideas lined up and we'll see whether I really can fly like a bird; well, not like Daedalus and his son Icarus out of Greek mythology, remember?" They both nodded in excitement. "Not like a bird either, our legs have the power."

"I bet we can do it, Arden," Hanna burst out with he juvenile enthusiasm.

I raised my eyebrows to indicate that I put its feasibility on a scale with doubt on one side and reality on the other. I already had made some drawings and put them on the table in front of them with explanations.

Three weeks later my thoughts and ideas had advanced enough to begin the new project.

However, an accident to Hanna, to begin with, postponed the project for some time to come.

Coming home from town one day, I was stopped by the Bonson children with grave faces. I was appalled when I heard the story. Hanna had gotten her right foot into the farm power mower and it was mangled badly in the process. Both parents had driven her straight to the hospital, from where the children anxiously were waiting for a word as to how severely the foot was injured.

It only had happened two hours before, so I decided to stay put. I couldn't do much good at the hospital; they probably had my young friend under anaesthesia and she wouldn't wake up for a while. I didn't have to wait for too long and Marg and Bill drove up and explained the situation, how much of the foot had been cut off and lost.

Marg did the talking. "They took the whole foot off, there was simply no way they could have saved it." She shook her head from side to side slowly. "She must have slipped to get it into the blades, she's always so careful. All our kids are. She hardly cried, Arden, in spite of the gruesome pain she must have had. You should have seen the foot; awful, just awful!"

I left the Bonsons with a heavy heart; next morning I wanted to join them to visit Hanna.

At home my mind immediately went to work, how best to make an artificial foot for my friend. I would put all my creativity and mechanical knowledge into that task. But, first of all, I had to know how much of the foot actually was cut off; her parents had only been vague about it.

Almost four weeks later, Willy and Hanna, with her crutches, came through the farm gate straight for the workshop. It looked like a warm spring day and I had the old barn doors wide open to let the bird voices and nature's fragrance unobstructed inside. They had seen me waiting in the open door. I was kind of impatient because I had had a dream, where I was shown how to best make an artificial foot for my young friend and what material to use. I was so excited about this project that I hardly took time to greet them.

I had made a drawing already and we three were bending over

it on and off. I said, "It's actually of a benefit that they cut your foot off a bit above the ankle, that way we can put a MT (Mind Tinker) into the upper part only to be used to lock the ankle in position. There are times when you need that. We will have to improve as you collect experiences." We had disconnected all the Mts again, having grown tired of their use. They had become kid's play, so to speak.

I wanted Hanna to know every stage and part of our enterprise, so that she would be able to build her own artificial foot later on. She still was in the growing stage and it had to be enlarged and renewed.

I continued the dialogue. "A very important factor is the weight, both feet should be exactly the same to walk in comfort. So, we shall establish that first. How do we go about it?" I asked them.

When I saw their questioning faces, I continued. "We do it by water replacement, get it?"

Willy's face lit up and he said, "We put the other foot into water and see how much it replaces. Then we weight the water and ..."

"You've got it, Willy!" I burst out, while pointing to the container on the floor I already had filled with water right to the top. It stood in a flat pan in which the spilled-over water would be caught to be weighed.

Our attention to the matter at hand was so intense that we hardly had noticed a man approaching until he was right upon us. He pointed a hand gun particularly into my director. Naturally, that instantly catapulted our awareness into this new and forceful development.

My first reaction was fear for the children, and while he waved us without any use of words out of the workshop towards the house, anger began to manifest in me; it took hold of my mind and heart. I would show him a thing or two. I was blinded to a nudge and a voice from within me. The anger put a vice on any thoughts of reasoning I should have had under these tense and obvious circumstances.

Inside the house the man said very matter-of-factly: "Get me all the food together here in the kitchen and pack it into boxes. Do it quick or else."

I was trying to stall for time and said, "Look, in the first place

I'm a vegetarian and don't have any meat at all." The next thing I felt was his gun in my face; more correctly, the impact of the gun he had wielded at me.

Then I heard Hanna's scream and again he hit me, but this time with his foot into my abdomen, so that I had to bend over with pain and fell to the floor. I heard him say, "Every time you scream and cry, he gets it." Then his cold-blooded voice called out: "Food!"

I heard Hanna and Willy hurry around and climb into the basement where I had some cans stored.

Suddenly I heard him barking at Willy and hitting him at the same time: "You do that once more and I'll kill you!"

Still on the floor with excruciating pain, I had seen Willy come up with only one can in each hand. Fortunately, next time he was smart enough to come up with a filled box, and a half minute later he appeared with a second one.

With five boxes lined up on the kitchen table, he commanded the children to stack them on the back seat of my car. When he saw Hanna laboring hard with a box and a crutch under her arm, he hit the crutch from under her. He must have hit her arm or hand because she cried out loud. He ran straight for me to boot me several times all over the body. I heard Hanna beg: "No don't, please, I'll be quiet, please don't."

By now I had lost consciousness, the pain was too severe and it put me out cold.

When I came to again, I heard a car pulling in front of the house and soon several policemen and first-aid or hospital men came through the open door. I wanted to say something, but my face was numb and I couldn't form any words. Finally, I got out: "Kids, kids?"

I heard the far-away voice of a policeman, "Don't worry, they are okay. They are both in the hospital already. Thanks to them we got to you."

Satisfied, I again lost consciousness.

It must have been much later when I awoke in a hospital bed with Bill Bonson looking down on me. "Gee Arden, I'm glad you made it. We had a few worries about you, with all the blood, you know." Then, "Just don't speak, I'll tell you everything. The kids are both here, too, Hanna's left wrist is smashed and broken when that crazy guy knocked the crutch from under her. Willy has nothing broken, but a lot of bruises all over."

I breathed deeply, I was so glad to hear my friend's voice and news. So what's a broken wrist? She's young and it'll heal anew soon. Suddenly I became tired again and Bill must have noticed, because he stopped talking and gave me a light tap on the shoulder with his hand.

When I awoke next time, it was dark outside and I was alone in the room. In trying to move my head, it felt awfully numb all over. Particularly my mouth, the gum, lips and the right cheekbone were in deep pain, kind of, hard to determine and to pinpoint. My whole face seemed to be wrapped with dressings and bandages; there were only openings for my mouth, nose and eyes. I had the strong desire to see myself in a mirror.

When I tried to move sidewards, I felt an agonizing pain coming out of my whole intestine and I feared that I was all cut up by this violent criminal. He could have been an escaped convict who had nothing to lose and who couldn't care less about somebody else's life. Before I moved again I tried to feel under the blanket over my belly. Thank heavens it wasn't wrapped nor did I feel any stitches. Maybe they still have to operate on me later. It sure felt like fire inside, like a strange entity, not belonging to me.

I tried again to move on my side to get out of bed. It sure wasn't easy, but I had made up my mind to go through with it on my own. Finally, I had my feet on the floor; at least, they and my legs were still in one piece. Standing up was hard and painful work and, while switching on the night table lamp, I only could drag myself toward the bathroom.

It was hard to believe that it was me I saw in the mirror; that head I saw looked simply terrible, strange, to say the least. Suddenly I had the determined desire to know how my face looked, in what shape it was in, if there was anything of the old Arden left. At that moment a nurse came in and called out: "Mister Hellmer, you are in no condition to get up," and she led me back to bed.

I would have replied something to her and ask questions, but how in the world am I supposed to speak? Never before in my life had I been so helpless, not being able to express myself. I indicated to the nurse that I wanted some paper to write on, which didn't seem to get through to her; she simply wanted me to lie down and relax. However, I was all worked up now and she must have felt my determination that I wanted to find out my exact condition.

After about twenty questions on the paper and as many answers back from her, I had a good picture of all my wounds and the remaining implications. First of all, I was glad to hear the my intestine was all right, I felt just the pain. X-rays had established that nothing was severed nor broken inside.

However, my mouth was in an awful mess! All the lower teeth (still my own) were gone. The gums had been repaired with tedious surgery. There were about twenty-five to thirty stitches in my right cheek; it had been ripped open by the impact of the gun. There were another ten or so stitches on my chin; the bone was not broken, although the pain from there was the worst.

The nurse was trying to tell me that in four weeks I would be like knew again, which I did not believe. She was trained, of course, to get the spirits up in us patients. There was no way to repair my mouth within a month or even three months. Nobody would keep me for a long time in this place with their kind of food intake. Yes, I'd better tell her that I'm a vegetarian. She tried to assure me that there were others with special food wishes and particularly the vegetarian dishes were made fresh every day in the kitchen.

"How am I going to eat a salad?" I asked. "Chewing is a very important process to me." She didn't have to answer, I could figure that out for myself. I would be eating their food, chopped very fine in a blender for the next few weeks. And what about my allergies? Would they consider that factor?

I felt so discouraged because I couldn't work myself out of this ... labyrinth, which it seemed to me. I was stuck! I would be depending on others for weeks, an even worse pain to me than all the physical wounds. At least, I wasn't depressed, a state of mind I loathed deeply.

For breakfast I sucked some lukewarm soup through a big straw. I was thinking of my carrot juice I could have had at home. Well, it didn't taste bad.

At nine o'clock, Bill was back and I heard the whole story from him. I had been right, that violent man had been an escaped convict. After he left me for dead, he had the children locked into the car trunk and driven off. Fortunately, Marg Bonson had seen him driving my car past their place and tried to phone me immediately, but there was no answer, of course. After conferring with Bill, they decided to phone the police who promised to come out as soon as possible. But it never came to that.

In the meantime, smart Willy, although under a lot of pain, had gotten the idea about the Mind Tinker hook-up, we still had not taken out of the car. In the dark he was able to find the switch, which when put on, automatically would engage the steering column lock -- unless kept unlocked with the mind.

So often we had driven he car with that mental discipline and exercise a couple or so years before, until we had grown tired of the experiment. As I mentioned already, all other MTs had been disconnected, but not this one in the car; out of laziness, I suppose. Well, lucky us now!

Willy was smart enough only to switch it on when he thought that there wasn't too much traffic to cause a serious accident, perhaps at an intersection where they had to stop. Boy, did he ever choose the right moment! When he flipped the switch and the steering locked in, the car rolled at once over the sidewalk curb into a power pole, and the police were right there.

Before the convict could collect his wits after that sudden surprise and draw his gun, two policemen already were upon him, because of the vigorous knocking coming from the trunk. What surprise was in store for them when the two youngsters appeared. Not one shot had been fired when the shackles were put on the escapee.

By now Hanna's wrist had swollen very badly and both children were under a lot of pain. However, they repeatedly told the police about me, the way I was left back, and actually they both wanted to go first to my farm and see whether I was dead or what. The policemen realized very quickly that they had two very determined young people on their hands.

After Willy and Hanna finally had the assurance that another police car with an ambulance was already on their way to my place, they let themselves be coaxed into the waiting ambulance.

Bill hardly was finished with his story when Marg and the two youngsters walked into the room. I would have liked to say so much, but couldn't, of course. My tears flowed freely and my emotions and heart went to them. I held their hands for a long time. Oh, did I love them!

* * *

Two days before this incident, I had had a dream, but did not put too much significance into its meaning. I had been walking in this beautiful and tranquil pasture along the shore of a little mountain lake. Suddenly I had this awful feeling of being watched by somebody very negative. Turning around I discovered a man with horns sticking out of his forehead. He looked exactly like the devil and approached me with a shameless grin. I didn't like him one bit and began to run, with him closely on my heels. When we came abruptly to a deep abyss, I stopped for a split second and then jumped in. It was a long fall and before I hit ground I woke up.

My immediate thoughts were that I could have jumped over that abyss; why didn't I? Why did I jump into that hole, where I might stay for, I don't know how long, if I survived the fall?

Thinking back to this dream I began to have an inkling of its meaning. Was it meant as a warning, if that's what it was?

Chapter 9
"Why Us, God?"

In between taking the bandage off my head, I had a good idea what my old new face would look like. There would be a long scar over my right cheek. The chin wasn't too bad. However, in order that I ever would be able to chew again properly, I certainly needed a good dentist to reconstruct and restore my lower teeth entirely. Perhaps I should get them all out and simply have a lower and upper plate, in other words, all artificial teeth. My lower gums still gave me a lot of pain, and I suspected a hairline break in the bone.

After three and a half weeks I seriously thought in terms of getting out of this hospital. My bandages had come off now and I began to hate their bland diet. Good vegetarian food? Indeed! What did those kitchen people know about my kind of intake? Or allergies? They were kind enough, though, to send one of their cooks up to me, to inquire what I exactly wanted and needed, after my bitter complaint, but I think she was more confused than before. No, it was no good; I had to get out and look after myself again with all the proper kitchen utensils available at home. Besides, physically I didn't pick up at all and blamed it on their food. Away from wheat bread, the only other grain they ever served was rolled oats. What about rye, millet, rice and buckwheat? And of late on the market, quinoa and spelt. Very important to us allergy people. They never served nuts.

When I revealed my intention to the head nurse, she immediately called the station doctor into the room. He began to argue with me as if I were just one of his ignorant patients. I almost got angry, but one thing I had learned in the past few weeks and that was patience. Respect for my fellow men, was another virtue I had begun to value; no matter how different somebody might be or what his opinion was. So I said very calmly and without any haste, "You see, Doctor, I know a bit about medicine, too, born out of the fact that I was given once the run-around by several of your colleagues. So, please, don't give me all that talk. Tomorrow morning I'm getting out of here, like it or not."

Well, I must have given them the right impression, namely that I was very determined, because they let me go without much farther argument. The stitches all had been removed, so I wouldn't be back and see them for some time to come.

I was glad to see my neighbor's face who had come to pick me up with his car. I even managed a grin, a feat still painful, towards the nurse, who had carried my little suitcase down to the car.

Oh, the fresh air through the open car window felt so good, like freedom. Of course, I had to go into the Bonson's place first and say hello to all of them and give them a big hug. When Bill wanted to drive me the rest of the way to my farm, I said, "No, Bill, I'm going to walk. It's something like a new life, I just have to get the feel of everything again on foot, the car is too fast. The suitcase is light enough to carry. And ... thanks once more, what would I have done without you?" I could see that they didn't want to hear it. What friends!

Already in the open door, I said, "Tell Hanna, please, when she comes home from school, that her foot is definitely next. She must be tired of her crutch by now. See you guys." Halfway down the road, I waved back at my neighbors with joy, knowing darn well that they all were watching me to see how well I was doing on my feet again.

* * *

After several improvements, we finally were able to put the artificial foot on Hanna's leg. It worked so good that it even astounded me, although I had seen it working in the dream. She got the MT inside her foot working so inconspicuously that nobody ever would find out what it was all about. It was goodbye to her last crutch.

To be prepared for any emergency, I suggested to my young friends to make a second artificial foot. This one would be a little bit different, namely it could be enlarged as Hanna was still growing. We had conceived this idea while we built the first one. It had been too late at the time to have this advanced concept still

63

implemented.

When they finally had it finished then, it worked so well that Hanna began wearing it instead of the first one we three had made together. I couldn't help but harbor some pride for my two friends. I had to stop calling them children because in so many ways they were adults already.

I was quite sure that there would be other improvements in the coming years; that's how we three were, we never stood still, it simply was not in our stars.

And, as it looked of late, our happy inventor and enterprising trio had been very contagious, because the Bonson family had shown their interests, too. Particularly, Bill came up with the most ingenious improvements for his farm work. Often, we all stuck our heads together for a brain storm. I guess the Mind Tinkers had initiated this new consciousness in my neighbors.

Unfortunately, our free-spirited inventiveness had a bitter aftermath a year or so ago because of the MTs we had so much fun with in disciplining our minds. Helen Bonson had married a young man, but their union didn't last. During the 'tug-of-war' over the baby later on, Helen's husband revealed the existence of our MTs to the press and for weeks we had reporters swarming all over to find out more about our secret gadget.

Now Helen and little Roi came over almost every day to look after my garden and clean the house here and there. I had little time anymore to do that. She loved gardening and it all grew extremely well. However, she also participated in some of our other ventures.

Finally I had my mouth full of teeth again, but only one-third were still my own. Chewing still was connected with some pain as if there were something haywire with my lower gum. The dentist assured me, though, that it eventually would fade away, because the damaged bone structure would take more time to repair, particularly since it was under pressure every day during the process of eating. Well, I believed him, but in the meantime I ate a soft meal more often than not to avoid chewing.

I also had found it very beneficial to apply to all my outer scars Vitamin E in cutting a capsule open and rubbing the oil over the old wounds. It did wonders! The healing it caused was unbelievable. When I saw my old hospital doctor again, he hardly could believe his eyes. When I told him about the Vitamin E treatment, he clearly showed doubts. So I asked him, "Then you tell me, Doc, what else healed my wounds so splendidly?" He just preferred to raise his shoulders.

One evening Marg phoned me with excitement in her voice and she asked, "Did you read today's paper already, Arden?"

"I usually do that at bedtime, Marg," I answered, "during the day I find so little time."

"Well, we can rest in peace now," she called out. "They killed that ... crazy convict right in prison, his own inmates did. It's right on the front page. So he probably ran against his own kind, too."

I have to admit, deep down I had some lingering fear that this violent man would make it a point to catchup with me again. Once these kind of people have locked something into their sick minds, they always come back to it, particularly when they have failed.

Of course, the questions have returned to me many times since the brutal encounter – why me? Why us three? Why had destiny put us onto such a savage collision with somebody we did not even know? Was there a connection behind the scenes of our lives? What were God's intentions with us to go through this awful upheaval in our peaceful existence? By now, I was fully aware of the fact that there must be some karmic connection with a past reincarnation.

To my pleasant surprise, the Bonsons also had taken interest in my spiritual pursuits lately, and all the books I had on the subject made their way down to my neighbors' place, to be returned with a lot of questions and discussions. There was not the slightest doubt in my mind anymore that we all had been together in some of our past lives; the likes and understanding we had for each other, it simply was there.

Just when we all had found our way back into contentment and happiness, another occurrence invaded our peaceful lives, which effects none of us could've foreseen. Willy's mother was killed in a car accident. Drunk behind the wheel, she caused a head-on collision, and the two people in the other car also lost their lives.

The Bonson adults and I tried in vain to find Willy and bring him for good to my place. I wanted to adopt him, but he was nowhere to be found – he was gone! Nobody had seen him or knew anything about him; he just left school, never to return or even contact anybody. He completely vanished out of our lives.

Naturally, we discussed Willy's disappearance many times, as he was like one of us. It simply was beyond us because it didn't make sense at all. He always had been happy in our presence, so why didn't he search us out for comfort and help?

I knew that my young friend had had a deep love for his mother in spite of her careless behavior toward him. It was a case of the son trying to help his mother rather, perhaps hoping that she would straighten herself out eventually. Willy never had any money in his box at my place. As soon as I had put something inside for his work he had done for me, like mowing the lawn, it was gone the next weekend, and he never used it on himself. I think he gave it to his mother.

The fact that two other people also were killed through his mother's fault, might have put a feeling of guilt into him, something like being responsible for her. It simply had been too much for him to handle and he ran away not being able to face us and the world around him. To where? God only knew. I hadn't the slightest idea. My heavy heart went out to him, thought, I wanted to help him so much, if he only had let me.

Chapter 10
The Wheel of God

Dreams had become so much part of my life that I could not imagine to ever do without them again. It was beyond me that not all people employed their evaluation and help, although dreaming often enough. Most of us take them rather in a light vein or let ourselves be upset by a nightmare. I strongly believe that at one time in our past we have lost contact with this so vital source of information and assistance, God assistance, that is. It should be part of the whole spectrum of our consciousness. We simply have turned too much attention to the material portion of our lives, which does not mix well with the spirit, as does water neither mix with oil.

However, this original connection easily can be restored, it's not something far away as we tend to believe. I've proved this, first with my young friends, who easily turned their dreams on again, in simply recording them every morning into a log on their night table. Of course, one has to make the motion before going to bed and to sleep, that one wants to become aware of his dreams and record them from now on. In the beginning there were times when I had five or six dreams during the course of the night and I used a tape recorder so as not to wake up too much in putting on the light and writing them down.

Another good example was the whole Bonson family lately, who joined me wholeheartedly in this venture, and we often enough discussed our nightly excursions into the spirit worlds, to get a better understanding of their meanings.

And how often have we heard of somebody daydreaming, appearing not to be present in his or her awareness. I know I'm in contact with something beyond my physical understanding when I do that, what one also might call an 'out of the body experience'. When I look for an answer to a problem, I sit down, relax and put my attention on the matter, and lo and behold it'll manifest in my mind. That's daydreaming. One simply gives Spirit, this God Force, an opportunity to help, to work for you, and It will if one believes in It and trusts.

The whole spectrum of dreams is a very vast subject, which includes the subconscious mind; Soul, this God spark we all have within us; Spirit or Holy Spirit, this God Force reaching us from the Supreme Deity, and not to forget those Entities I like to call dream Masters or dream Friends, whose real position was still a mystery to me at the time. Today I happen to know that they are a group of Adepts, spiritually highly evolved. They are there to assist us in our struggle to create a link again through our dreams with the spirit world, where we'll meet them as our guides. They will link us up with the All-embracing Force, which we have lost.

At the time I wrote this, I was not much more than a novice, but had learned to work myself into it with diligence; it kind of came naturally to me and I wanted it, of course, unlike some people who are afraid, if its beyond their physical or mental understanding.

The following dream is the most extensive one I ever had and if I wanted to write down every detail it might take several chapters. So I only shall account for the important portions, all connected to the people in this book and it will put some light on our different activities and relationships of love and hate. No interpretation is necessary about any part of this movie back in time around the eighteenth century and the actors, the roles they played then and are playing again today in a karmic interaction.

* * *

During this incarnation I was put into the body of a boy in 1749 in the Port of Spain on the Island of Trinidad.

England, France, Spain and Holland played for power and possessions around the Caribbean Sea to establish colonies. In this kind of environment and atmosphere, piracy was flourishing.

One day my mother virtually had been dumped in the harbor by pirates who had no use for this Spanish woman anymore, after having abused her for months aboard their ship. My father, a Frenchman, found her near death when abandoned. He took her to his shack where he nursed her back to health again. In those days women were scarce in the Caribbean and their eventual marriage was nothing outstanding. I was the oldest of five children.

My father's hard work at the waterfront barely brought enough income for all our hungry mouths to survive. Early we children learned to work, and, more often than not, opportunities produced young thieves, but our parents were glad when food came to the table every day, they did not inquire or even care from whence it came.

My name was Raymond and at the early age of fourteen I had left home to face the even rougher life of the sea. I grew up to be tough and intended to make more out of my life than I had experienced so far under the wings of my parents.

My first job was on a sailship, the Tabago, a reasonably fast vessel, if not the fastest in these waters. Captain Cough knew nothing of the virtues; he ruled with the rope and his cruelties to some of his men were well known. No seaman in his right mind would hire on twice with a captain having such reputation.

I tried hard to please the ship's master and his men, but they took more joy in beating me rather half to death. There were days when I was not conscious of my surroundings with excruciating pain all over my body and even then I was kicked and mishandled by the crew like an animal, to let out their anger and frustration.

In the first few months I was never without bruises and pain from the beatings and the captain outdid them all. Rarely did anybody last longer than a year on the Tabago.

Every ship was equipped with cannons and every man at sea had his sword and dagger. The ships with the most guns and the highest speed were the safest. For the others it was more or less luck to survive, for danger was waiting often over the horizon.

I had outlasted every crew member and was on my fifth year under Captain Cough. I had grown into a strong young man. Now my master thought twice before he still would dare to try the rope on me because I easily could've stood up to him in strength.

The reputation of the Tabago was well known throughout all the Caribbean harbors and it had become increasingly more difficult to find and hire men for her crew. When we came from Cuba this time, we had the most vicious looking men aboard. Often the captain used me in calling out, "Give that wild-looking creature at starboard there the rope, Ray, I'm too busy here." What choice did I have but to obey. I always made it a point to say,

"That was the captain's order; next time you might do it to me." One practically could feel the hatred of the men.

One evening below deck during mealtime, heads were stuck together in groups. I could feel their apprehension about me, so I said, "Look, you men, I'm as much of the crew as you and I don't get any favors, not from that bastard, I tell you. If that devil tells you something you'd better do it or else, unless, of course, you should have the desire to go against the devil himself," I laughed. "I'm with you, I can fill my spot."

"How do we know you're not the captain's man?" I heard a voice from out of the dark background. "You've been quite a while with him now, we've been told."

"I can see that my words mean nothing to you," I replied with shrugging shoulders. They didn't trust me, but neither did they trust each other.

For four days Captain Cough's reign of disciplined cruelty went on until one night, when it happened, I was overpowered, bound and gagged. Then they got the devil himself and tightened him to one of the masts. A new captain took command with all the rougheons cheering him on. They untied me then and brought me face to face with my old tormentor. He shouted at me: "You young bastard, I knew it was you behind this. You'll pay for it, you'll pay for this!"

I leaned toward him, laughing and spitting into his face: "You old goat, I should've beaten you to death long before this as you've done with many. So they finally got you." For a moment I felt sorry for him, but not for long. I took him by the hair, bent his head back and spit in his face again, accompanied by the laughter of them all.

The new captain's name was Ramsey, but only two of his old friends called him that. To the rest of us he was 'Guts', because he had had the guts to take over the boat -- it had been his courage. He approached me and said, "Good that you are not with him, but you beat up old what's-his-name and I think he should have a chance to give it back to you." All agreed.

So I answered, "What would you've done in my shoes? Did I have a choice? I can see, though, your minds are made up already. If he wants to get even with me, give him a rope and let me have it. I won't even lift a finger." For a moment they were speechless, then they cheered the fellow on to go ahead.

I finally fell lifeless on deck; however, this incident left something in the back of their minds. Some carried me below to wash my wounds with water. In a day I was on my feet again, still weak, but feeling much better after a hearty meal.

Although our ship was a fast sailer, we only had six cannon and the crew was much too small. As we would capture other vessels, particularly the ones from overseas whose crews knew nothing about the dangers of the Caribbean waters and had only little weaponry, we intended to add to our arms and fighting men. Everyone was looking forward to capturing women and our talks about them were endless.

I also learned how they had tortured Captain Cough slowly to death, then tossed him to the sharks. Nobody had any kind of scruples on this ship. At times, I had a funny feeling toward these cruel men, but it never lasted too long; I would stand my position.

Our first fat ship was an English supply vessel whose captain was a greenhorn in these waters and so was his crew. Before they suspected anything we had boarded them and it was under our control without any fight at all. We unloaded the booty onto a little island, after we had gotten rid of the crew in a small boat on the open sea. Then we burned their ship to the water line to make it worthless. Only three of the crew had joined us and they were Chinese.

We had plenty of all now; booze, food and more weapons, but still no women. We had one big party on our island and drank ourselves half to death. This was the life we had been waiting for. After a week, captain Guts finally got us on our feet again by putting all the spirits under lock. He perked us up with the words, "Now we're going after girls. We also must find us a better island to hide on." Thus, we set out to sea again, singing and laughing.

Not too long hence we sighted two heavily armed Spaniards, but didn't dare to get close. Our by now ten cannons and thirty-three poorly trained men were nothing to be proud of. We were not hard up; after all, we had enough to eat and drink for months. Besides, most of the islands in the tropics had plenty of fruit trees for fresh supplies.

One day we came upon an island in the Bahamas where they just had landed hundreds of slaves from Africa, but they were guarded by armed men who refused to give us some of the women. However, we returned during the night and silently overpowered and killed the Spaniards. Their muskets were a

71

welcome addition to our arsenal of weaponry. In the morning only the young girls were herded aboard and the rapings began in full view of everybody -- like animals. I had my very first girl under the laughter of the older and much more experienced men.

Finally we found a perfect island near Jamaica for hiding, where we unloaded the girls and hid part of our booty; this would become from now on our steady base. From here it was better to continue our piracy. For days we had orgies of the flesh and got drunk at the same time, only to sleep it off for a couple of days and do it all over again.

One day somebody said, "What about white women, these blackies are too easy." We all fell in like wolves and cried out: "White girls, captain, white women!"

So we left the black girls behind and set out to sea again. We changed our ship's name from the Tabago to the 'Windy Girl', because our reputation had gotten around and they were on the lookout for us.

Proudly I stood at the wheel and watched the sails in the wind. I was able to edge our ship even faster into the wind so that the water sprayed over the bow. Suddenly, we heard the shout of the lockout from the top of the mast: "Boat ahead, boat ahead!" That brought Guts and the rest of the crew on deck. Who would it be? What was their flag?

It was a French vessel, so, soon our French flag went up, too. In two hours I had the Windy Girl almost alongside to see closely how well they were armed. It was decided to go for it. By now I was an expert in getting us close, unsuspected at first, and then move over quickly for our men to jump in surprise. At the same time I had to drop the sails and throw our lines across to lock our vessels together.

In this case it worked out as expected, but the French were well-armed and fought splendidly; they were excellent swordsmen. Finally, I was able to swing over, too, being the last because of my job as the helmsman. I swung my sword left and right, hitting and killing. The French lost their gallant battle, but not before eighteen of our men also had lost their lives. We never had any second thoughts about the wounded and remaining sailors, overboard they went, a feast for the sharks.

In a week our two ships had made it to our hidden cove on the island. New supplies, but no white women, and some of our best men dead. For weeks we tried to lick our wounds with drink and

Negro girls. I hardly knew anymore what I was doing, I had lost all sense of time and value and was in a state of stupor.

One morning I picked myself up and walked along the beach in the fresh wind. Thoughts crossed my mind; is this what life is? Other thoughts welled up, but I like it, I've all I want. What better is there? If there was I didn't know about it. I became mad at myself to have thoughts like that; was I afraid? Flashes like this went through my young mind, but they never took hold.

After our wounds had been healed and our passions satisfied, slowly we sailed out to sea again. Our crew had become much too small to tackle anything of importance. The English now had warships in the West Indies, and soon the other countries would follow suit, no doubt.

One day Captain Ramsey had an idea and he talked it over with the rest of us. "We have become too weak to attack even the smallest vessel at sea. How about getting ourselves some seamen from the harbors. We could go ashore at night and search them out from the taverns. There are plenty, I bet, waiting for an opportunity to join us."

"It'll work, Guts, it'll work," I called out. "As long as we avoid the Port of Spain and the surroundings, they are bound to recognize us there."

In Haiti I found myself another steersman with lots of experience and he brought with him a friend. We three eventually became very close comrades, as if we had known each other all our lives. Their names were Arthur and Chuck.

As our ranks filled again, we made plans to look for a new field of action around the Panamanian Isthmus (named so today). Maps were very scarce and inaccurate, so we discovered everything by 'wait and see' and surprise. Another hiding place was found on one of the San Blas Islands with no natives living on it.

Our first capture was a Dutch merchant which was easy picking and lots of goods came our way. They had two white women with them, but, after abusing them, we lost interest, they were too plump and lifeless. Since they didn't put up a fight, we let them go. Our holds were full again, but we had nothing to drink.

We liked the new hideout, but had to capture a suitable ship first to get the black women and the spirits back from our old retreat.

"Ship ahead!" came the call from the top of the mast. "Two ships ahead!" he shouted after a while. Then, "Three ships ahead!" Captain Guts scratched his head. Should we pursue them? One could be a ship of war and it would be much too tricky. But the temptation overruled reason, so we followed.

It took all night and close to dawn we almost had caught up. Suddenly we discovered that we had company behind us; he was a fast one, too, a good sign. There was only one way to find out his identity, turn around quickly and swing around again parallel to him.

At calling distance, our captain shouted over: "We are from Trinidad, from whence you might be?" We had our port cannons ready, just in case. Some of our men stood with the muzzle loaders at the ready, hidden.

"You seemed to be following the three merchants," came their answer back. "Have you business with them?"

"We might if the price is right," was Guts' answer.

"We also have interests in their holds and we set the price," came over the water. "But three ships are hard to bargain over." Then, having waited a minute or two, "Two for us, one for you."

"Ho, ho, you sharks," Guts called back. By now we all knew that we were facing fellow pirates. "We were first so we have first choice, unless you want to feel our guns," and Guts gave the signals to raise our gun doors. We now had sixteen cannon, eight on each side. That did the trick.

"Take your pick, we're satisfied," came their answer. "We'll take the last one."

As we began edging closer to our prey, having hoisted the British flag first, the Spaniards became nervous, more so when our pirate's flag suddenly went up. Some of their muskets rang out, which was a big mistake, because now their lives wouldn't be worth a damn anymore.

The boarding was done quickly and some of their heads were chopped off. One whole ship was full of young girls, future wives for their colonies. We certainly had our hands full now. However, there was no booze aboard.

In all this first confusion, none of us had kept an eye on the surrounding sea. Two English warships had closed in on us. A broadside of their guns on the other pirate's ship finished them off and ripped us very quickly out of our present state of happiness and lust.

When Captain Ramsey grasped the situation, his commands were loud, swift and fierce. We jumped on board our own ship, cutting the lines in the process. With half of the sails still up, it didn't take long to hoist the main sail. The wind was reasonably good and we were off. One of the Britishers was close enough and their cannons spewed their destruction upon us. We were hit several times and some of our men lay in their blood. With no guns in the back, there was no way to answer their fire. Two of our masts also were hit and toppled on deck, but it didn't diminish our sailing power very much.

At full speed now we had reached enough distance that they had to stop shooting. Fortunately, we had been quite a bit faster than our pursuers. That was a close call all right. We only had three dead men and the masts easily could be repaired. While laughing about our luck, the three comrades were dumped overboard for the sharks. This was the pirate's life.

In two days we caught up with a French merchant, that was filled with French liqueurs and wines. We only lost two of our men while boarding. The two beauties we encountered went one to the captain and the other was determined by card games between the men.

Over two years later and not many of the old crew had survived. My two friends, Arthur and Chuck, were still around and we three had become inseparable. As a fighting threesome during the boarding process we had become a reliable force to be reckoned with and had the respect of all, including the captain's. Guts had lost one of his eyes and his old friends. He was very irritable now and lost his temper too easily. Except for enough women, we had everything and rested often for three weeks at a time on our island hideaway and 'heaven'.

Three large merchants had been sighted, but we didn't like their looks and let them go. This was already in the 1770s, and most of the sailboats were well armed now. We decided, though, to have a closer look at the fourth one, which trailed a mile or so behind. He was English, so we raised our English flag and pretended to be just a sleepy sailship passing, going a bit faster.

I stood at the wheel, yawning. Most of the crew pretended to be asleep. I shouted over: "Ahoy, sailors from back home! Did you have a good passage?" The very moment their sails blocked the breeze into our sails, which inevitably slowed us down, was my signal to turn the wheel and slam our ship into their starboard. But they had been warned and were ready to defend themselves as quickly as we jumped and swung over.

Often executed, our attack worked as planned. The Englishmen were well-trained, though, and knew how to use their swords. Swinging over as the last one, I saw my two friends in trouble and rushed to their assistance. Out of the corner of my eyes I had seen Captain Guts go down and seeing him in his blood made me furious. I fought like the devil.

When I saw my two comrades go down within a short time, it ached my heart and also raised my guard for a second too long. An officer's sword penetrated my body; it was the end.

From far above, I still was given the opportunity to observe that my pirate crew was able to overpower the Englishmen eventually, but the cost was stupendous! More than half of the men were lost.

* * *

For days I walked around in a daze after this dream. Had I really been that violent, so heartless and so cruel to the many peaceful and unsuspecting people? I finally came to the conclusion that there was a good reason to give me this terrible dream 'full blast', so to speak.

Now I understood only too well, why a curtain is drawn over every past life. Only Soul knows. Got in ITS mercy has arranged it that way. If a young child is coming with this kind of a memory into its new life, it might very well become insane. Many of us had this kind of a violent past, called for by our karmic debt, a drama none of us can avoid. The physical environment is Soul's training ground, involving thousands of lifetimes or incarnations. The wheel of birth and death seems everlasting, until we pull ourselves out of this merry-go-round with soul- or self-recognition.

Anger! The trouble to control my anger at times must have originated out of that pirate experience and it almost cost me my life now. If it wasn't for the anger I entertained toward that escaped convict, I would've gotten out of that encounter much easier, I'm sure. The vibrations of anger are picked up easily by people, particularly if they are on the same band also, and the reaction is often instantaneous -- which equally might apply to love also, although not all the time.

I was grateful, though, that the many other passions out of the pirate's life had no dominance today anymore, I must have worked them off. The time under Hitler and my participation in the war might have been big factors in their eradication or neutralization.

And who had been all the actors out of that incarnation? The Bonsons had been my French-Spanish parents in the Port of Spain, and some of my siblings from then are today's Bonson children, with the exception of Hanna. She had been my good friend, Arthur, while Willy had been Chuck, the other pirate friend.

Captain Cough, who gave me the cruel training as the young boy, today came back into my life as ... well, he got back to me as the violent convict, trying once more his brutal art on me and perhaps also go get even. I bet that the men who murdered him in prison were some of our old pirate comrades, who I don't know, of course, because I've never seen them.

Our karmic debt always comes back to us in one or another form, until it is paid for or worked off with the good virtues. It never fails! Some lessons go back for thousands of years, until the right life comes along for Soul to either learn or wait for a further opportunity to balance the karmic scale. This is the law of the Supreme Being, the law of Cause and Effect, or the law of Love, the Wheel of God, as I like to call it.

Chapter 11
The Dream of a Boy

Almost every day I had to think about Willy – if I only knew that he was all right. After the last dream I felt even closer to him. So we had been good friends as pirates and even died together. I began to understand some of the struggles he had had with his mother, a struggle of wanting to love and be loved and to belong. What kept him only from turning to me in his emotional plight? Oh, I longed so much to have him with me.

Sometimes I also caught myself looking at Hanna longer than I should. No, I would not reveal this dream to her, it would stay in my own private collection for the time being.

During the following dream I was not aware that I actually had it. When I woke up in the morning I remembered it, though, to record it and try to make some sense of its meaning.

* * *

It was in a movie theater where the projector put a movie on the screen without any pictures at all, but the viewers were very attentive as if they actually saw a movie rolling past them. The back of the theater had many rows of boxes on top of each other, all filled with people also watching the movie. However, the higher one sat, the more one was able to see the screen, but only the viewers in the top boxes saw the whole spectrum of the movie. While the masses sitting in the many rows below only imagined they saw everything and were happy with it, the people in the top boxes, in actuality saw the picture in its fullest range, or in its truest sense without obstructions nor illusions.

In the next segment of the dream there was a train rolling past slowly and many men, mostly young, stood outside, holding up

78

their thumbs to hitch a ride, but the train didn't stop for them. Some, however, jumped on simply to get a ride and the rest were left behind.

Still another segment showed the young men left behind; some of them looked rather like boys in their teens, as they clustered together to decide what to do next. They were met by a rather wild-looking bunch of 'kids' who had lived this forsaken life already for years. Most of them wore long hair and unkept beards. The two different parties began to mingle and walked out together into the wilderness, away from civilization.

And again another segment showed this bunch of young people again, where most of them had adopted the habits of the untidy group, and almost all looked dirty now, with long hair and beards. Well, not all, though, some were sticking out as strong individuals they did not submit to smoking pot and taking drugs, to give only two examples. Although they might not look much different from the others on the outside, their inner strengths were unbroken. Eventually, they were the ones who would find their way back to civilization.

* * *

I mulled this dream over for half a day and when I sat down in my workshop to contemplate it, I came up with the following explanation:

The situation in the movie theater showed the different levels of consciousness of us human beings. While the masses of people, who sat in the lower rows of the cinema, imagined they saw something on the screen, only the ones in the top booths were able to see the real 'McCoy' of life, the full spectrum. I was entirely free to join either group, which seemed odd to me since I already had vast insight behind the scenes of life, comparable with the top boxes in the movie theater perhaps.

Sure, the message of this dream for me came through now; I'm still too much of a doubter because I let myself go in not trusting this ... Force or Spirit. What other proof did I want? I had so many insights into <u>all</u> life and knew about karma, reincarnation and believed strongly in their validity. And yet, I let myself go. My emotional hang-up about Willy was a good example.

That brings me to the next dream. Willy, at the moment weak with pain over his mother's death and on top of it feeling guilty over her having killed two other people through the accident, had been one of the young people standing outside the train, trying to hitch a ride, but it didn't stop nor did he jump on. In other words, he was not able to get back into the normal life of society (the train). So he joined the others who eventually wound up with the dirty bunch and intermingled with them, even looked like them and took part in their negative activities, like smoking pot and taking drugs.

However, some stook out in spite of the negative environment and they were the strong Souls; nothing ever would get them down. Their survival factor was way above normal and, having grown much stronger, they eventually would get back into society. Yes, I believed with all my heart that Willy was one of them. We had been buddies over two hundred years ago as pirates, now I was sure and had the distinct feeling that my young friend was as strong a Soul as I was. He would make it and we two would see again.

I finally said to myself, "Come on, Arden, smarten up. If Willy has the strength to pull himself out of his morass again, you surely should have the strength, too, to pull yourself away from your emotional attachment to him. Remember, old boy, as Soul, he is old already and might even be more mature than you are. You don't own him, so set him free."

Well, I did, grinning to myself. The dream had taught me a lot. I had plenty of faith in my young friend now and was very confident.

* * *

Emotionally rejuvenated, I was ready to pursue my next project, namely to build a self-propelled glider and keep it aloft with my own muscle power.

Although Hanna was the main participant and helper in building my 'artificial bird', often Helen helped also and the whole Bonson Family dropped in, here and there, to see how we were progressing. We discussed it often, as we did about many of our other involvements, too, as if we were one big family.

All over the world they were building these flying machines and actually flew them already, using human muscle power. However, my design was different, because I did not want to use an undercarriage, instead I would be using my own legs.

My project would have a very light wing with a bulgy plexiglass fuselage in the center. From there I ran steel pipes to the back to hold the tail section with the elevator and rudder. The propeller was mounted on top in front and above the legs, because I would be doing the pedalling lying backwards with all the steering done by my hands.

There were doors in the bottom of the fuselage with very light sled-like tracks for emergency landings mounted on them. So far this was not too much out of the ordinary. The revolutionary new idea I implemented into the design was two wing halves on top of each other, so that I was able to change the wing profile during flight for very slow, but also fast speeds. If I put my two hands flat against each other, it would compare with the fast flight, but cupping them a bit or even more, gives an idea how the wing profile will look for a slower speed. I had developed a system to lock in the wing halves as sturdy as if in one piece.

Since this design did not permit the ailerons on the back of the wings, I put them on the wing tips together with small 'flip-ups', as I called them, aids for a slower landing, to interrupt the airflow, if necessary.

The main idea was to carry the whole contraption on my shoulders with straps, run down a hill or against a strong wind, then swing my legs into the fuselage quickly, to put my feet on the pedals to get the propeller going. The doors would be closed under me, of course. Beside the glass dome on top, there also would be windows to the sides of me in the wings, so that I was able to see below the glider. I always would be staying in this lying position on my back, since there wasn't enough room to sit upright; besides, I had designed it to do the pedalling in that particular position.

There were many changes as we proceeded with the building, as often transpires with a new project, we also took our time to find the right material and at times had to send for it as far away as Germany and England.

Although the name 'Windjammer' is originated from the olden times of sailing the seas, I gave my glider the same name because, to me, it meant something similar, still having the dream of my piracy in the back of my mind, no doubt. Windjammer simply sounded right to me and that's what I painted on the wings.

Nobody could hide their excitement as the first day of flight approached. I had taken up steady exercising to be in top shape for this event. I wanted a strong wind for the first flight to have all the right conditions in my favor. The Windjammer weighed in at eighty-six pounds, not too bad to carry on my shoulders. Of course, the weight would decrease drastically as the wings began to lift the craft. And for the landing I always could keep my legs inside the fuselage and land on the sled-like tracks below the doors.

The day had arrived! There was a little hill behind the pond and we had mowed it so that there were no obstructions for my running feet. Everybody was present and Hanna and Helen helped me get the Windjammer on my shoulders to be strapped on. After I had closed the plexiglass dome over me, they let go of the wingtips and I tried to get a feel of the different steerings in the fifteen-mile-an-hour headwind. It amazed me how light the craft was already in the breeze and I hadn't even moved yet.

Running then down the hill I was airborne in ten steps. With my feet on the pedals I got the propeller going in a jiffy and I began to rise ... yes, I did rise! I heard them cheering from below.

I was so jubilant, so ... words failed me. I was free like a bird, yes, I was free! I had done some glider flying during the war in the German Air Force, but this was different. Here I was the master and could stay up ... perhaps all day.

I must have been two hundred or so yards up and swung around over the farm again, where I could hear their joyous shouts from below. Oh, what an event! If only Willy could have experienced this, too.

I had dreamed about this since my early boyhood when at the age of ten I already had begun to make my first drawings. But all had laughed about my idea and attempts, even my teacher. Later, in the Air Force I had discussed it with close friends, but nobody believed in its feasibility. My persistence, insistence and belief had paid off now, I had been right all along. Oh, I was so proud that I had proved all those doubters and ridiculers wrong. But all the Bonsons had believed in me; what friends! I just loved them.

In two hours I came to the bottom of high cumulus clouds, not in pedalling all the time, though. After I had reached an up-draft in perhaps half an hour in the air, I had taken my feet off the pedals, which automatically disengaged the propeller so that it could rotate freely in the wind. As I circled slowly in the up-draft and rose higher and higher, I eventually touched the base of these clouds.

My shivering reminded me that I was not dressed for these heights of a mile plus. So I descended by changing the wing

82

profile to faster flight and less lift. I had to get back to the farm. Where was I anyway? I had drifted towards the Rocky Mountains and saw the vast forest below me, which had been in the easterly direction. Well, navigation had never been my trouble and not too long hence I sighted our two farms in the distance.

When I landed against the wind, I came to a halt on my legs with only five steps. Lifting up the dome, immediately I was engulfed by a hundred questions and a thousand words. After I had let the Windjammer down, my two assistants, Helen and Hanna, brought it into the workshop so it wouldn't blow away and be damaged. We all settled down near the house, where the women had prepared a welcome lunch. I was hungry, but hardly got a chance to get my food down – there was simply too much to tell and talk about.

"If only Willy could have been with us now," Marg said with a serious face. "The boy was so much involved in all this."

"Yes, you are right, Marg," I agreed with her. "I had a dream, though, a rather private one, letting me know that he is all right and can fend for himself. It told me to let go of him, emotionally. In any case, I'm sure we'll see him again, much more matured."

For a few moments everybody was quiet, thinking about our young friend. He was in the heart of all of us. However, the conversations slowly picked up again.

Having satisfied our stomachs, we all helped to get the dishes inside and clean up the tables. When there was a lull in all the talk, I said, to put their thoughts on a new concept, "Eventually we all will fly the Windjammer, of course, it's not just for me."

For a minute or two their words failed them, as they looked at each other for something to say. Then it broke loose and I heard Marg's voice, "No, Arden, not me; I'm too old for that and haven't the knowledge to fly. Besides, I'm too fat, ha ha, I wouldn't even fit into that thing. No, not me, ha ha."

We all had to laugh about her comment and I could see the enthusiasm of the kids; to them it was very easy, of course. Then I heard Bill say, "You think I could ... I'm strong, you know." He scratched his head, the idea had to sink in first, and I could see that it did, faster than the subject permitted.

All afternoon we talked about it and discussed the many questions every Bonson member had up his or her sleeve. The situation had changed somewhat, they all saw themselves flying high above now.

When I was alone with Bill for a moment, he whispered, so nobody else could hear him, and he did it with a wise grin, "You know, Arden, I dreamed about it, I mean not in my dream during the night, and I thought often if I could do things like you do, and now I already do, as you know. Boy, I'm going to fly that ... Windjammer, too, if it's the last thing I do."

I whispered back, "The last thing, Bill? It'll be the beginning of only one new venture you'll never forget. There'll be many more, Bill, many more."

He stroked his chin with delight and nodded with satisfaction.

Chapter 12
More Than We Bargained For

My next flight was on a day without a trace of wind to prove that I could start and keep the Windjammer in the air without nature's assistance. I ran down the little hill again and had no trouble whatsoever to stay aloft. Then I tried the same again in not using the benefit of the hill; instead, I just galloped along the flat ground. Although I had to run for a distance of about thirty-five yards before I could swing my legs inside and pedal 'to beat hell', to keep me from touching the ground again, I was able to stay up and rise higher, to get out of the 'gravity bubble', as we learned to call it later on.

Every week I held regular flight classes with all the Bonsons to teach them the fundamentals of flying first, but it also included some understanding of the airfoil and why it was able to keep an aircraft in the air. The one with the most questions was Bill, who also came up with the suggestion to build another Windjammer to give everyone a better chance to participate and find out first-hand how it worked and was done. What a splendid idea! Then we eventually could travel with two of us over the vast wilderness of the Canadian forest.

One day I stayed up for nearly ten hours; the conditions were perfect all day to use the continuous cumulus clouds for my uninterrupted climbing and descending, using the up-draft created by the towering clouds. The only time I had to use my muscle power and the pull of the propeller was to get off the ground. Away from that, I simply used my craft as I would an ordinary glider.

This time I had dressed properly, but became increasingly hungry as time marched by. When the golden sun sank beyond the horizon, I came down on the landing spot of my farm without the use of my legs this time, I simply was too numb. We had to find some softer material to lie on for the future.

Only Helen was there to help me out of the Windjammer dome. As stiff as I was, I walked a few steps, with push-ups in between, to loosen up again. I said to her, "Tomorrow it's your turn, Helen, if the weather stays like this. Don't tell anybody; we'll surprise them when I go down to your place and you'll be in the air, okay?" She agreed with a broad smile, of course.

This was only four weeks after my first flight and they all had heard enough of talk, advice and warnings, too, from me. Helen and the two oldest Bonson boys, Rick and Herb, would be the first to give it a try. The other two – one of them, Hanna – still were too young. And Bill? Well, I wanted him to choose his own time.

As I suspected, Helen was off the little hill against the five to eight miles headwind with ease, and had no trouble staying up in the air. On her way back overhead, I waved and gave her the go-ahead signal as we had agreed upon.

So I took her little son, Roi, and walked down to the Bonson farm where I met Marg outside. She greeted me with the words, "So you took Roi off Helen's hands for a while. I'm so glad she's with us again, Arden. Here, among us, the boy is safe and sound and can grow up in peace."

Then she detected the Windjammer high up overhead and burst out: "Who is flying that up there? It's not Helen, is it?"

I simply nodded slowly with a knowing grin.

Next I heard her shouting at the top of her lungs, and running at the same time behind the house: "Bill! Bill! Boys! (The other two children were at school) Look up there, it's Helen!" Both of her arms were reaching high up. "Helen is flying it, see, up there." Then she came back to me, still excited like a little girl.

Soon Bill and sons came zooming with a tractor off the field to join us. Wiping the sweat off his forehead, he said, "That girl, she's good, isn't she? Look at her, going higher and higher?"

Then I heard Herb and Rick asking, "Are we next, Arden?"

"Of course, next weekend, if you wish," I answered. "Let's ask your dad, though, with all the farm work right now."

"Sunday will be okay," Bill said. Then he banged his flat hand on my back and continued, "Although our farm comes first, of course, I often think that all things we do go kind of together." His wise grin indicated that there was a double meaning to it and I understood him. There were so many improvements on his farm now, that the olden days of hard work did not exist anymore. If they wanted to, they could've taken a week off without serious effects. And almost every month they added a new gadget to simplify some work process.

The glider with Helen only could be seen as a speck on the horizon now and the men drove back toward the field again, while Marg smiled and parted with the words, "I'm not going up, Arden, if you still should have your mind on that."

I simply grinned at her, then took Roi and walked back to my place. The little fellow always was so quiet and happy, I never heard him cry once. Sometimes I wondered how he was related to his father through past reincarnations? Already there had been some kind of violence in his young life without him actually being aware of it. Or was he? After all, Soul is adult already at any stage of It's life.

Five of us were flying now and the second glider was in the building stage. It was the job of the children under my guidance, here and there. With that kind of experience they would have a much better understanding how an airplane was put together and how it worked. Besides, I didn't have the time, having my mind on other inventions.

However, Bill dropped in often enough, too; he was not to be left out, because he wanted to be able to discuss every detail with his children. I remember the day when he made his first flight, which he did not do before he was good and ready.

His daily exercises had loosened his muscle tone; after all, already passed the forty-five mark, a farmer's work is not all that multilateral anymore, from the viewpoint of balance. The night before he phoned me and said, "If the weather is right tomorrow, Arden, I want to get in my first flight. I think I'm in good enough shape now." He was six inches shorter than I with my six feet, but weighed about forty pounds more, mostly raw muscle, I suppose.

It was on a Saturday morning and everybody was present. First I had him just running with the Windjammer strapped on his shoulders, to get the feel of the different steerings. Then he ran down the little hill and swung his legs inside the fuselage, closing the doors behind him, to land a moment later on the sled-like tracks.

He became too anxious, so I said, "You better relax, Bill. You

87

want to rest a few minutes?"

"I know I'm too tense, but that's all you get out of this old farmer, Arden," he laughed. "No rest, please, I want to go all the way now."

Well, maybe I wanted him to be too perfect, so I made up my mind and called out: "All right, Bill, you know yourself best. This is the real thing now. Let's go!" and I pointed down the hill.

If my farmer friend was too tense, he didn't show it because his flight was indeed perfect. He had not the slightest trouble climbing and he stayed up for nearly two hours. He even used his legs for the landing. I had to laugh about Marg, the way she went through all his flying and landing maneuvers with different movements of her body, arms and hands like a young and agile girl, as if with him in the glider.

On the ground again, she ran toward him and called out; "Bill, you made it! Oh, you should have seen yourself. How was it? Tell me, tell me!"

With the exception of Helen, the three men flew only on weekends because of their farm work. I still took to the air occasionally and only helped when needed. My mind was too occupied with other 'things'. When I had my attention on a new project, I couldn't be bothered, not even with flying, my old love.

One day at noon, Marg rang me up and said rather excited, "There are a couple of reporters here and they asked whether I had seen anybody flying for hours with a glider over the country. What do I tell them? Once this gets out, can you imagine what that does to our peace out here at the end of the road?"

"I was afraid of that, Marg," I answered. "Sooner or later they'll find out. Of course, somebody was bound to have seen us, and you know how people are to get their names in the paper. We'd better do it right, Marg, to get rid of the pests. Send the two over. Tonight we'll talk about how we're going to handle the situation."

So Helen brought the two reporters over. Quickly I had taken the Windjammer out of the workshop, to close and lock the two big doors. No use to let them see all the other things I had in there. One of them was a seasoned reporter and he suspected at once that this was not an ordinary glider with a propeller on top to keep it in the air. In order to make them rather believe that it was not much of an unusual flying machine, I offered to fly it for them, so that they were able to see it first-hand.

Later on, however, I had honest doubts whether I did the right thing. My intention was to take the edge off 'something big'. Those people always look for an exciting story where there is none. But it seemed that the exact opposite was the outcome.

The newsmen simply had blown everything out of proportion and the result was that for weeks we had reporters from all over pestering us and there wasn't a thing we could've done about it, unless we wanted to hire guards and spend a lot of money.

What had we done? The Windjammer certainly wasn't something so outstanding to start all this. Every night the Bonsons and I sat together to make plans for the next day, what to do and to say, so as not to make them even more suspicious. Somehow the Mind Tinkers also were mentioned again, as if some kind of a negative entity was digging deep to get us out of our peaceful existence. It all was too strange to us to understand.

Finally I had a long distance call from the States -- a magazine asked whether they could come for an interview? I thought that that might do the trick. If a well-known publication gives a detailed account of the Windjammer, it might put the whole affair to rest.

The Bonsons already had been pestered by cameramen and TV crews, so this time I made sure that the people from that magazine visited only me. I told my neighbors to stay on their farms as if they had nothing to do with it, which came close to the truth.

They came with two interviewers and two cameramen. Fortunately, they all were real professionals, not pesty or bothersome. Of course, I had to fly for them several times to demonstrate the Windjammer's capability and maneuverability.

Then I got the idea to let one of the reporters fly also, because he was an experienced glider pilot. Within half an hour he was in the air and enjoying himself tremendously. Our liking for each other was mutual; those people were not looking for high drama and their report was honest.

Their magazine article later on must have done us a lot of good from every point of view because the news media stopped coming and we had our peace again.

If there was an outstanding lesson to be learned out of this episode – and it was not trying to hide anything so visual as the

Windjammer – that there always was somebody 'wise' lurking behind the corner to get the press into action and their own name into the paper, and these people are quicker than one can hide.

A few weeks later Bill Bonson told me, "I'm going to put a fence right across the road, if it's all right with you, Arden, and the proper sign goes beside the gate. I know that the road is not ours, but who knows and who's going to challenge me?"

"I'm with you, Bill," I agreed, "and let me pay half of it. After all..." That's as far as I got.

Bill shook his head vigorously and said more seriously than I had expected. "No, Arden, all the things we got from you already. No, that's our baby. You've made new people out of us, so let's give something back, if only a fence with a gate to match."

Well, this was not quite the end of the story either. A government inspector drove up one day and wanted to see the Windjammer. So I led him into the workshop; it was too late now to get the bird out. He had a good look around, of course, and noticed all the other things I was working on. If he had any thoughts, he didn't express them. He asked, "How fast does this fly?"

"Oh, I would say around thirty to thirty-five, not much more," I answered. "You can fly it if you wish," I added, presuming that he had his pilot's license.

He just shook his head and suggested, "You need a license if it flies over sixty miles. So don't fly it that fast," he grinned.

"It'll fly apart at that speed," I answered.

He believed me without an argument. Then he looked at the other one we were building. It was still not covered with cloth and the ribs were visible. He looked at it extensively and nodded, smiling. I guess the boy in him liked what he saw. "An excellent job. I read some of the reports. Something good they taught you in the German Air Force."

Before he entered his car he said, "I guess the press had their 'fun' with you. Don't worry, I won't add to it." And he drove off. What a relief!

"Who was that?" Marg phoned as soon as the car had passed their house. "He had a government insignia on the door. Don't tell me they are interested in the Windjammer now?"

"No, Marg," I answered with a grin to myself. "I think he was our insurance valve for our old peace again. A little bird must have whispered into his ears, too, and he liked what he saw."

"Oh you, Arden," she laughed out loud, "I know you are kidding me, ha ha. See you."

Chapter 13

A Painful Interlude of Old Karmic Ties

My bookshelves were overloaded and I either had to store some of them in boxes, get rid of them or build new shelves, so I began looking through all the old ones -- did I really want to keep them?

Flying saucers, I had well over a dozen of them. Since my dream experiences, almost all that knowledge had been overhauled; well, not all. So I leafed through them and got stuck; certain things were rather interesting. This new old curiosity led me to the next dream.

* * *

When I woke up I was in a dream, although not knowing it at the time. I saw somebody sitting on the ground in the grass at my little pond and I recognized him at once as a space traveller. He greeted me with a smile and I liked him right away. He introduced himself with, "My name is Vetus."

I said as if I knew, "I guess you know my name."

He nodded and answered, "We know about you, what you are doing, but it's safe with us. We would like to expand your consciousness about the physical universe. Being here at your pond with you does not mean that our bodies are of the same vehicles you are wearing most of the time."

At that moment it dawned on me that we might be in the dream state.

We had started walking toward a road leading off my farm into the woods. I asked in a questioning-knowing manner, "You mean we're in our astral bodies now?"

"You see, that's what I would like to discuss," he answered, "and also show you. We are not in the astral medium at this moment."

His answer puzzled me and questions romped around my mind, so I burst out, "I know I'm in my dream state now, but ... I ... if not in the astral, in what state are we in then? Soul?"

He smiled only, without giving an answer; instead, we marched on until we came to a clearing where he had a small spacecraft parked. Gesturing toward it, he invited me inside with the words, "I suppose you don't mind a little ride?"

"Not at all." I must have sounded overjoyed.

We were met and greeted by two others of his companions who took the controls and off we went. Not too long hence we arrived at a place, which, when entering, I surmised was a huge space ship. I was astounded over its dimensions inside. Naturally, I had a hundred or so questions I would have like to shoot at my guide, but nothing was said as we slowly walked along a gang plank with a handrail on one side. At its end we entered an elevator, going down perhaps a dozen floors.

Finally, we went into a large room, which looked like an oversized living room. About fifteen people were present, some of them seated, and conversing with each other. It was a completely relaxed gathering, as if this was their home.

With the exception of two, none paid us overly attention. A man and a woman greeted us with broad smiles and she said "I'm Zine and my partner here is Vektor. We three are from the planet Venus."

Their looks were blond with steel blue eyes and perhaps four inches taller than my six feet. The others presented four or five distinctly different races, some dark-skinned, and others might have been up to eight feet tall. They clearly gave the impression of a high intelligence, but not in a demonstrative manner.

"We thought that you might like to know more about us," Zine continued, after we had seated ourselves on easy chair and a couch. "Your thoughts are still with us in space occasionally, as you call it. Perhaps we can help you to reach a new concept about our world out here, which lies above your Earth and which your astronauts are trying to reach now with their rockets."

Their smiles were continuous, it seemed, even while they

spoke. Vetus said, "I mentioned the physical universe, when I met you in the beginning, and I detected your questioning face. Until now you only have been introduced to the Astral World and their human instruments, away from your own environment. However, there are several different stages or layers in between, not known to most occult and metaphysical researchers on your planet. We are in that category; we are not in the astral form."

His revelations really surprised me. They gave me a lot of opportunity and time to think, and when I was just about ready to ask a question, one of them would continue their explanation. This time it was Vektor who spoke up. "It is a matter of vibration and sometimes the borderline is very fine yet distinct, not easy for an untrained eye to see. There are several stages in between the physical and the pure astral environment and their instruments, but all still belong to the physical category. On Venus, where we three live, you people from Earth could not exist, although we are still classed the physical creation. You only could visit us with your Soul bodies, and many of you do, to be taught in our spiritual institutions and temples."

After a long pause he continued, "With your awareness level you are way beyond the masses of your fellow beings and it is not for us to further your spiritual consciousness -- other beings do that. However, in a way, our assistance might also be of help in your spiritual quest."

Then Zine said, "It might be of interest to you to know how different our two environments in actuality are. We become much older than you do. I'm three hundred and nineteen of your Earth years old, to give you only one example, because our vibratory rate allows that kind of life without great effort on our part."

When I heard Vetus' voice again, he said, "Well, did our explanations put light on some of your outstanding questions? I shall think so. Perhaps you also would like to know that we are not the initiators of this experience for you; it was arranged by your ... whom you call 'dream master' or 'dream friend'. Often these beings ask our help and that's why we are mainly stationed here and in other parts of this solar system. So, we might see you again some day or not. We will go now."

We shook hands and their warm smiles sent me off. Of course, this time I had an even closer look all around -- if I only could stay for a while longer and be shown this enormous space city! If Vetus picked up my thoughts, he didn't let on. In a few minutes we entered the small space craft to fly back to Earth, where I soon thereafter found myself in bed again.

* * *

The first questions to myself were: What happened to Vetus and his walk back with me to the farm? What about the time factor? We had left in broad daylight during the dream and now it was still dark outside. Well, I relaxed again; by now I knew that a dream master can do anything with you if it helps to further your spiritual progress.

I sure liked that dream experience because it was somewhat part of my physical environment and life, and it cleared up a thing or two.

Now I knew what I would do with all the flying saucer books, get rid of them; perhaps a library had use for them. I had been trying to hang on to an old 'thing' I actually didn't need anymore. At one time it had been something like a stepping stone toward my present awareness. And I bet that's why I was given this space experience, because I had leafed through the UFO books again, with some interest trying to manifest once more. In any case, my time was too precious to indulge in the past.

The other important reason for this dream was to establish the position and relationship of the diverse physical worlds, wrongly put by me into the astral realm.

* * *

For two and a half years, Bill Bonson was trying to convert into organic farming and this was the first year where they didn't use any chemicals or artificial fertilizers. The market for this kind of produce was getting better every year, but the changeover was difficult and a challenge. They also had cleared another twenty acres for an orchard, and that's where I was helping them. The trees already were planted and I tried to hook up a little computer on the dripping system.

A large holding tank in the center would supply every individual tree with water and the right nutrition at the same time. I had seen this in southern California and convinced my neighbor that that was the ultimate way of future farming and offered my help.

"Financially, I'm in a deep hole right now, Arden," Bill said with a dry grin, "but not for long, if it works, as you say, together with all our other changes and improvements. However, when I see all the other gadgets you built ..." He didn't finish his sentence and I knew very well what he meant. With other words, his trust in me and my technical know-how was complete.

The Bonsons had thrown all their weight into this latest way of farming, after having talked it over with me extensively. But I still could see and feel some apprehension about their venture; would it work? When could they expect the first return? The money-time factor was so important.

I knew by now that I would be wasting my words, and our friendship perhaps also, to offer them financial help. Bill was too proud for that. However, I tried to help with other means, like hooking up this computer for the watering system. It kind of bothered me, though, that I couldn't be of more help; after all, I had started the stone rolling, more or less, with my ideas of a natural life, which required to a large extent organically grown foods. I also had spoken of the vast pollution of our foods through sprays and the overuse of artificial fertilizers, causing many sicknesses. First I had brought over one of my magazines in which all this was explained extensively. Of course, I hadn't talked them into it, but my words had helped a lot in the matter of making up their minds to change their farm to this new concept of agriculture.

* * *

One day, unexpectedly and without writing first or giving me a phone call, my daughters from Edmonton came for a visit. They both were finished with high school now, wanted a change of climate and stay at the coast for the winter season, at least.

However, our old closeness was not there anymore, probably due to the years of separation, we hadn't seen each other for over six years and hardly corresponded.

Naturally, I offered my assistance. To begin with, they stayed for two weeks at my place and I introduced them to the Bonsons. I was very disappointed though that they showed so little interest in our gliders and the other things I did in the workshop, but we had a good time hiking in the wild forest.

When my daughters became restless, I knew very well that they wanted to be on their own, soon move into Vancouver and find a job. I helped them getting a nice suite and within a week they both were working. I was surprised that it worked out so well, they really wanted to give it an honest try to make a go out of their own lives without parental assistance.

I decided to give it a sincere effort to get my girls better to know again. When I was in town I dropped in for visits and a friendly chat. Unfortunately, however, my positive outlook began to fade slowly. They associated with people, particularly young men, I could not be at ease with. I simply could not see eye-to-eye with their new life. I seriously wondered whether I was too old-fashioned. Was I still living in my old German shoes, so to speak, and the old consciousness I tried to escape from, with so little tolerance and love? Because of that my marriage didn't last and went to pieces eventually. All that was still very vividly in the back of my mind and now catapulted to the forefront again.

And other questions romped through my mind, had I contributed to this? After all, I had been part of their upbringing at one time. Or was this their mother's upbringing? In spite of our original differences I could not believe that, she had been a very good parent.

Perhaps I didn't understand young people anymore, being all cooped up at the end of the road and so little experience and contact with them. But what about Hanna and Willy? We three had a very close relationship and a wonderful understanding with each other. Of course they were still younger and not continually with me. Neither did they grow up in the middle of a big city, where the pressure of their peers was perhaps more intense.

Then I began to wonder, with the new insight I had today, whether our karma called for this? Perhaps we had been together in our past lives. Well, my next dreams bore that out up to a certain extent.

* * *

I was led back into Spain during the medieval times. Born to a wealthy landowner as a boy, I was the only child who made it into adulthood.

The priests and monks of the local church and monastery were a power-wielding clique who used fear tactics to keep their coffers and collection boxes filled and have the simple people submit to work for them. It was a very one-sided affair.

However, they never could've done this without the support of the Lord of the castle and the province. He owned much of the land and often enough the people also. He and his family were very pious, bordering on ritualistic black magic.

The only bright light in the dark spiritual atmosphere was my father, a wealthy landowner, who had to walk a very narrow line to keep himself from being swallowed up by either the church or the lord of the province, the Master of the castle. It seemed a continuous power play among them. Early in life, my father taught me already what one might call the 'diplomacy of survival', the meaning of which was to walk the middle path between the peasants and their work they also had to carry out for the aristocratic Lord and the church. This kind of power play in using the helpless people was seldom in our favor.

The Master of the castle had three daughters and we met at certain events and festivities for the rich, where the next up the hierarchy of the state and church joined often for their intrigue behind the scenes. Fortunately, the powerful bishop was my father's older brother, who became often enough also our protector and savior.

If I would have chosen one of the Lord's daughters for my wife, it automatically would have ensured our protection and freedom of this so often painful dominance. They all were much older than I and we had no likes nor love for each other. During the festivities of the upper classes we met, socialized and talked, often working ourselves into intense frenzies of mockery and sarcasm, pretending to be pleasantries.

My uncle, the bishop, spoke often to me and my father, to bring about a union with one of the three daughters of the Lord, but our hatred was too deep and we despised them, something we never could show openly. In fact, I never could've married another girl, because it would've been a sign of disrespect, enough reason to cause our downfall.

So this play went on for many years and I never chose one of the three daughters or refused them openly; I stayed single for the rest of my life because I had no choice.

My ex-wife and two daughters of today had been those three daughters of the Lord in the medieval times in Spain.

* * *

During the next dream experience (second dream) most of the same actors were together again. This time I was the adopted son of a family in one of the larger cities in the south of Italy, about two hundred years after the reincarnation in Spain. My parents had been drowned in a boat accident and my uncle and his wife had adopted me very reluctantly. Only because I was thirteen years of

98

age already and soon would be on my own anyway, made them take me in.

They had two daughters (my daughters of today), ready to be married off, but their behavior and way of life made them poor prospects for any decent future husband. My uncle drank a lot and was most of the time under the influence of alcohol; while his wife (my ex-wife of today), who had no love for me, tried to keep her daughters in line. She was terribly vain and the three of them stuck their heads together all day to plan on how to best attract suitable men.

However, during the evenings and the nights, they lived a different life, men from all parts of society sneaked into the house and into one or the other bedroom to indulge in their fleshly pleasures.

Having come from a family with high moral standards and good ethics, I was appalled by their behavior and felt extremely uncomfortable living with them. The three years I had to stay were pain and frustration to me, leaving deep imprints.

* * *

For the next incarnation I, as Soul, adopted the body of a girl (third dream same night) about a hundred years later in the same Italian family. I was one of seven girls and they were as different as they came. My father was a strict Catholic and made sure that his daughters were brought up well with high moral standards and a good education. My mother (my ex-wife of today) was of a lighter side and it often caused controversy and an upsetting atmosphere, particularly to me because I was a 'papa girl'. Two of my sisters (my daughters of today), the oldest ones, always sided with mother and her needling of dad. But they also took pleasure in taking it out on me, the youngest one.

This going up and down the scale of virtues and passions was quite upsetting to me and tore on my innermost emotions. I believed deeply in the goodness of my dad's life and what he stood for. However, I grew up with part of my mother's and part of my dad's imprints also. End of dreams.

* * *

Obviously, some old karma still was not dissolved and it had to be worked out in this present life. In any case, my daughters and I had a good 'go' at it again and those three dreams made me breathe easier once more because I believed that I had learned a great lesson out of our encounter, namely emotional detachment. This time I did not hang on to them with my most inner feelings, as I had done years before, when I finally was able to tear myself away from them in coming to the coast. I didn't like what my daughters did nor the people they associated with, but I still loved them as souls.

Physically we also were separated again by a long distance when they phoned me one day that they were on their way back to their mother. There they had perhaps more security and a better job waiting, as I understood them. Well, it also made me breathe easier again.

Chapter 14

A Visit to the Source of Inventions

I've had many dreams I cannot write about because they are only given for me and very personal. To the spiritually awakened person particularly, it is important to be very discriminatory and disciplined and not -- as it is the common custom in our society today -- go left and right and expose every detail of one's spiritual experience to everybody. This kind of deed can have painful effects on the person who does it and, on top of it, might expose the listener and receiver to some powerful metaphysical inside knowledge he or she is not ready for, so suffering is the result.

Increasingly I've learned to respect those beings, entities or whatever one wants to call them, who belong to an exalted spiritual group of Adepts. Some of them are guardians of Wisdom Temples on the different spiritual planes or here in our physical universe. I happen to know that one of these temples is located in the capital city of Retz on the planet Venus, which is still considered a physical environment, yet not visible to us here on Earth, as we know by now (dream in Chapter 13). I don't feel right, though, to be led and to converse with nameless beings I've learned to call dream masters or friends. We here in our western world are so used to naming everybody, that if I can't tack a name to him or her, I feel uncomfortable because my mind is programmed for names. However, I've been assured several times that names are insignificant and irrelevant. We cannot use our physical faculties when we proceed in our quest for spiritual enlightenment.

In order to give due respect, though, to the beings I meet in my dreams, who have vast God powers, knowledge and wisdom, and who guide and help me to reach a high spiritual understanding, I shall begin their names of dream master or friend with capital letters from now on. Anything or anybody related to the Supreme Deity, like Spirit, Soul or the Masters I spoke about, should be in this category. That's how I feel anyway.

* * *

More and more I was shown in my dreams advanced technical and scientific achievements – 'achievements' to us on Earth that is – and I was at a loss whether I should follow them through as an inventor and sell them with a good profit. Not that I needed the money, neither did I think that our society with its present state of consciousness – having little discipline and only material gains in mind – should be exposed to a revolutionary new invention. My feeling about it was very strong. But why was I shown this technical data, if not to give it to my fellow man for his benefit?

Often my thoughts lingered on this subject ... it was perhaps a lure of a kind. Sometimes the physical environment is not what it seems to be and our mind can be deceptive; one has to learn to judge things differently.

The Japanese and Germans were working on trains without wheels, where a magnetic cushion was used to run the cars along a track at very high speeds. However, they were expensive projects, needing special tracks and using a lot of electricity. In what I've seen during my dream, all this was unnecessary.

* * *

When I became aware of my surroundings, it was in the Astral World. I knew it because I had seen something similar before. I had been given into the care of a young man of perhaps thirty years, but I knew already that the people here actually were older compared with our Earth time.

He had my height and wore western clothes, as I did. He introduced himself with, "I'm an engineer, one of ten, who is respon-sible for the upkeep of the transportation system in this large city. There are different kinds, of course, but at the moment we're only concerned with the earthbound conveyance, as you would call it."

We had entered a car or bus and he pushed a button to get it going. As it picked up speed, it gradually lifted off the ground. There was no pilot or engineer running this vehicle. He explained, "This particular bus follows a decided invisible magnetic-electric line and I could not change its path. From high above the city I'll show you first the layout of our system."

The tracks throughout this enormous city seemed to be faintly lit and appeared like a vast net, spanning every district. There also were lines leaving this net, leading into other cities and parts of this country. Shortly thereafter, we came down again and to a stop, where we entered another bus, which stayed on the ground this time. Their stops or stations were only small, nothing like any of our train stations, perhaps a bit larger than a bus stop. This seemed to be their sole commuter system and it was all automatically controlled, as we run our elevators in large buildings.

The next vehicle took us to a central underground station from where the electricity was fed into the different lines and my guide was telling me that it was low voltage, similar to what we use in our telephone wires. It all looked very simple, compact and comparably small.

Using a very fast train, we came to a huge building, the famous Astral Museum. Every imaginable invention of the future is already available and exhibited here. I had been here before without my knowing it, taken by my Dream Master. Almost all inventions on Earth are originated here and received in the dream state. This fact is only seldom known to the inventor.

My escort showed an identification card at the entrance and we went straight to the hall and the item of interest to us. There I was shown the mechanical-electric-magnetic works of a car in its simplest form and how it worked in relation to the tracks. Some transportation had two tracks, some only single ones, while others were underground or overhead. It was up to the inventor how to go about it or what worked best in his particular case. The knowledge and concept of the technician or engineer played vital roles in the shaping of the new creation. My next awareness was in bed, awake.

* * *

There are many millions of miles of train tracks spanning our globe and they could be used as is with low voltage put to them. Then, magnetic trains without wheels would have to be built to replace the old coal, diesel and electric engines. However, every individual car had to be supplied with this magnetic propulsion system -- one of them could not just pull a long line of coaches. Yet, in spite of this and in its simplicity, it could be done very inexpensively with no comparison to what we have today. Much pollution could be eliminated and accidents from bad tracks were practically nil.

This invention, if I wanted to call it that, intrigued me so much that I decided to build a small model and run it around my property. Instead of tracks, I wanted to use two parallel copper wires, something easy to come by and certainly easy enough to run all over the ground, only to be pegged here and there.

One evening – it was winter again with a lot of snow this season – we were sitting in the Bonson living room and discussing this project. Bill said, "You know I was offered railroad tracks, the narrow gauge they used to use in underground mining; over three miles of them. Wouldn't they be perfect for that? Of course, I wasn't interested."

Instantly my ears went up and I said, "Wow, three miles, hey? What did they want, Bill?"

"Not much to speak of," was his answer, "I remember him saying that he just wanted to get rid of them, for the price of the iron, I guess."

So I was able to lay my hands on just the right tracks and even could build a larger engine for people to sit in and to be operated from the inside. I was as excited as ever to begin my new venture. We had decided to start one end of the tracks all the way down at the Bonson farm, that way I had a straight run of over a mile.

* * *

In the meantime, however, the second youngest Bonson boy, Bill Jr., had become old and tall enough to be trained for his first flight with the Windjammer. The other glider was finished, too, by now, but we still hadn't named it until Marg phoned me one day and suggested the name: Venturer. It had been her idea alone and we adopted it gladly, although she probably never would fly it herself.

Spring was on he march again and Bill Jr. was ready as ever. The start had been rather easy for him and I could see Hanna's face when her brother glided over our heads. Of course, her longing was with him up there, being the last of the youngsters. I also wondered how much her foot would be of a hindrance during the run.

We already had test flown the Venturer and now Helen took off after her brother, to fly together for an hour or so over the country. The cumulus and their updrafts still were missing at this time of the year, so they had to use a lot of their muscle power to stay aloft.

Well, they only were able to fly twenty or so minutes; without the help from Mother Nature, it was too arduous and they simply ran our of steam. But Bill Jr. did okay and we all congratulated him on his first accomplished flight.

* * *

Helen came more often to my workshop than anybody else, and it was not to watch me, but rather to work on her own project she had going. She had discovered that there were toys to be invented and a good market for them. Having sold one already, Helen was looking for a broader field rather, with her eyes on all of the children of the western world. When she had the prototype of her latest creation finished, we all complimented her, it was that good.

Of course, I helped to get it patented, which was rather difficult because of the overrun market and its diversity in that particular bracket. But she insisted and waited patiently for the confirmation with the document from the government patent office.

Some inner voice, as she was telling us later, had urged her to go for it. I think it had bugged her quite a bit to live with her son off the parent's pocket since the divorce. She simply wanted to contribute more to the Bonson household besides her labor.

Suddenly, the young mother had a good enough income to live on her own if she wanted it. At the moment, however, she had no intentions of leaving and there were no reasons to begin with, but she put some money down on a house. Needless to say, Helen's parents were very proud of their daughter and so was I. It looked as if our atmosphere of inventiveness had inflamed and infected another one of us and it made us feel extremely good.

* * *

Whenever one of the Bonson tractors was available and free, I made it a point to put down and screw together some of the narrow gauge tracks. It actually was easy work, but it would take a considerable time, to get the three and a half miles down. Occasionally one of the boys helped with the second tractor and by early summer it was all done. I had decided to run copper wire along the tracks for a better conduction. Now I put my sole concentration into the magnetic-electric system of the enterprise.

It was a busy time for all of us and when I had the feeling that intensity had crept into my work, I simply took off and flew a couple of days, a marvellous tool to put my 'innards' back into balance. I don't know why I wanted to push so hard to get this project done. I also went down to the Bonson farm for a week here and there, offering them some much-needed bare-knuckled labor and enjoying it.

Going on fall, I had a call from a southern California outfit which had bought one of my inventions; something had gone haywire and they were pointing the finger at me. Well, I actually appreciated a change like that; the flight down south I saw as a challenge of a different nature; it would do me good.

Chapter 15
"Without Love You Would Not Exist!"

That professional people who work for a big firm and with a degree and several years of university behind them, can be so ignorant, so ... well, actually I shouldn't say that and accept my fellow man as he is.

However, I had flown to California to this large company which complained bitterly about one of my inventions they were using on a regular basis. And what did I find? That they had replaced some parts with second-rate ones, although I had specified only to use the very best. I already had dug deep into the back of my mind for some mistake I might have made. When I showed them the manual, their red faces would have been enough apology as far as I was concerned. I finally was able to wiggle myself out of there again, because they really tried to go out of their way now to make up for their mistake.

So I rented a car and visited some of the famous sights, like Hollywood, for instance. Then I went to a beach in Orange County where I had been before and loafed around in the sand for a week, playing volleyball with the locals. They didn't mind having me, so I couldn't have been that bad.

I made up my mind right there and then that I should get away for a month at least once a year. This different atmosphere put another perspective on my consciousness and it was for the better. One easily can engrave himself and resist a healthy change. The balance between the micro- and macrocosm might get out of whack.

I finally decided to drive the four hundred miles to San Francisco, instead of going by air. I never liked to drive long distances, but here was another opportunity to break up the old mental patterns a bit. I took three days and enjoyed it tremendously. A different side of myself was revealed to me and I began to like it.

After half a day of business, I drove along the inner city of San Francisco to decide what to do next. I wondered about the many young people who practically lived on the street, singularly and in groups. I talked to a Negro woman who slept every night beside my hotel entrance. All day she was pushing a shopping cart, filled with her sole belongings, searching through garbage cans to find something to eat and useful items to sell. She was very reluctant to speak with me, and turned over on her meagre bedding again, glad that I continued my walk up the hotel stairs.

I though about her for a long time and inevitably Willy came to mind. Where was the boy now? Was this his way of life, too? Where did we as society fail? Did we take the wrong turn somewhere along the line in the past? Or are these the times of today? Devoid of love and compassion?

All heavy questions I was not able to answer, and they lingered in my subconscious mind until I fell asleep, only to become aware that I was in an odd and strange land.

* * *

I saw a thousand different monuments and statues all the way up to the horizon they also were behind me and left and right as far as my eyes could see. Perhaps there were even more than a hundred thousand, all representing images of famous people, animals, beliefs, religions, philosophies and consciousness, to name a few. All of them were encircled by people, walking or even running around and around, as if attached by invisible threads or some magnetic power.

First I came upon Abraham Lincoln; it was a huge statue, with him sitting on a chair with dignity. It seemed as if millions of American people walked past him again and again, looking up to him, as if he still were alive.

The next monument was that of wars; it also had a tremendous size and it was revered as if a living entity. I saw politicians, businessmen and old soldiers actually kneeling down and praying for its survival, while the overwhelming majority of the population shouted slogans to eliminate the wars.

The monument catching my eyes then was not because of its

huge size, but its dark, red color hovering above like an aura, and it was that of anger. I was even able to feel its vibrations for miles away and there was nobody smiling among its worshippers, who also maintained strong connections with many other monuments like invisible strands of steel.

Then I came upon the twin pillars of pro-life and pro-choice and observed a lot of controversy. I sneaked up to see who actually had the better argument. One thing was for sure, the pro-choicers wouldn't be there if it weren't for their counterparts, who had a strong connection to the anger monument and much backing from there. I heard a lot of quotations from the Bible, but one particular one made the most sense to me, it was Genesis 2:7, where it says: "And the Lord formed man of the dust of the ground and breathed into its nostrils the breath of life; and man became a living soul." There was too much fanaticism for me to stick around for very long.

My next encounter, in the truest sense of the word, was with the rock-and-roll monument. Its quivering height disappeared right into the clouds and the people praying to it acted as if in a trance. It felt inhibiting and even destructive to me. The connection to their 'god' was strong and unnatural. I had to get out of there fast because that kind of music always was irritating to my consciousness.

The following thousand or so monuments were puzzling to me. They all represented Christ, but every one was particular. It was, when I had a closer look, that the concepts about their saviour had developed into all those different images, some are as adverse as day and night and very fanatic about their belief. It struck me as odd that only one man, namely Jesus, should have started all this.

When I encountered the many Buddha monuments later on, although quite individual in groups and understanding of their savior, there was none of this severity, but rather a gentleness and tolerance toward all other religions. Here I did not feel the uneasiness, not that it was of my taste.

The worst of all the monuments – and most worshipped with a deep severity and often animalistic behavior – were the ones pertaining to drugs, like alcohol, nicotine, pot, opium and cocaine, to name a few. Among them also were the statues of caffeine and even foods and drinks. They all had to do with addictions, of course, a pest growing by leaps and bounds in all of Earth's societies today.

This district was so uncomfortable and even upsetting to me, that I looked for some relief, but wondered whether there was any to be found among the many monuments, statues and images of philosophies and religions our world population is adhering to. One I found with the old Greek philosophers like Plato, for instance, but his statue was so small and not easy to find. However, it emitted a strong spiritual vibration to the people walking around it.

Love, I wondered, where is the statue of love? It should be the largest of them all. But there was none. I was disappointed. Are we that low into the negative passions and activities that love has no room among us anymore?

Finally, I had grown so tired on my walk through our world's societies with the many inhibitions and outweighing the positive side of the scale, that I refused to go any farther. I had had enough of it!

Suddenly, I heard a faint, deep-throated and rolling laugh; it grew louder and louder into a thunderous, earth-shaking rumble, which shook the hell out of all the monuments and statues, and me, too. But all held fast under the screams of fear of the millions upon millions of people and worshippers, to their relief and comfort.

I still could hear the terrifying laugh in my bed and it jolted me into a sitting position. "Who was that?" I called out in dazzlement, wondering where I was for a moment until I got my bearings. It was in my hotel room in San Francisco. Then I heard the quiet chuckle of a laugh and the words: "That was your negative mentor; you wanted to know where your society had taken the wrong turn. Can love be formed into anything solid? Into a monument or statue?" My Dream Friend had sounded the words and asked the questions, then he added, "Without love you would not exist!" I craved for more of his utterances, but none came.

* * *

Too awake to go to sleep again after this dream experience, I sat until dawn to record it all into my journal and to tutor my mind with its meanings.

Actually, there isn't much to explain -- that dream was very self-evident. We, as society, but individually also, have created everything the dream demonstrated at one or another time, to the point of worship and idolizing, and are still doing it. Good or not, the old images prevail in spite of their negativity and destructiveness, like drugs and wars, for instance.

Well, not me, I was telling myself, and if I'm a worshipper of any of those monuments, I shall drop them and change ... yes, change to new and positive images. The last thought perked me up and I decided to see some of the city's beautiful sights I knew about. Cheerfully I went down to the restaurant for breakfast.

* * *

With a map beside me on the car seat, I drove through the inner city first to begin my tour. Although the dream had put a new light on our society's pains, well, like the youngsters I saw sitting on the sidewalk there right now, a feeling of helpless wondering still was with me.

It was Sunday and the traffic scarce, which gave me an opportunity to slow down and not rush past the old and new buildings and store windows. I was even able to stop for a moment or two and have a closer look at the people who had made the outdoors of this big city their home, living between the cold stone walls of the high-rise from one day to another, hoping for a handout here and there.

Some inner urge made me park the car and walk along the sidewalk to see them closer first hand. Then, an inner power stopped me, and, as if in a trance, I looked from face to face of the youngsters, sitting there in a circle. Some had their upper body parts exposed to the sun. My eyes rested on a boy, not older than fourteen, fifteen or sixteen, it was hard to judge. He was hardly more than skin and bones, but his face looked matured. His eyes ... I <u>knew</u> those eyes ... I <u>knew</u> the face .. It was Willy!

I stood there transfixed with a pounding heart. My mind raced to, I don't know where. In my thoughts I formed the name, 'Willy, Willy!' A young man approached me and asked for some change, so I gave him two quarters.

Suddenly, all the others had turned their heads into my direction and Willy, too, looked at me. At that moment our hearts and souls locked into each other, and it was simply indescribable. I could not move, but my young friend arose slowly, as if in some pain, took his meagre belongings and walked in my direction. My eyes began to water when we stood for a moment face to face. My next awareness was that I had my arms around him, and we held on tight. It was such a relief.

His friends had surrounded us and made offensive remarks, like, "Come on, Willy, don't get soft on him," or, "Get some cash out of him, Willy." So Willy took his bundle off his shoulder and gave it to them without a single word. While they had a fight over it, we two walked to the car, followed by their shouts and cries of insults.

Inside the vehicle we looked for a long time at each other and clasped our hands. Under a faint smile he stated matter of factly, "I never will go back there again."

There were not many words between us, it was not necessary; the inner understanding and love was there. He did not want to go into the hotel with his awful clothes and said, "They wouldn't let me in, Arden, I know." So, after a search we finally found a cheap store open where we bought it all new. He insisted on having two sets of underwear, to dispose of the one he had put on for the moment, and one after a bath, the first in a month. I had to smile inside.

While Willy sat in the tub really enjoying himself, I tried to get some light vegetarian food for him. His stomach would be revolting against anything rich. I remember from shortly after the war, when loving parents killed their homecoming sons, having been in Russian prison for several years. When I saw him climbing out of the water, there was not much meat under his skin. I could see that he was weak with only little balance. Tomorrow he would have to see a doctor.

Before he began to eat, I suggested, "Try to chew a lot, Willy, and swallow it slowly. It'll take time to get used to even a light vegetarian regimen again,"

"Don't worry, Arden, I'll listen to you," he answered, setting my mind to rest. "You're smart, the smartest man I've ever met. You've taught me a lot of discipline, yes, I remember, and I'm not on drugs. All the others are and they always kidded me, but I said no." I don't think he said that to flatter me.

That's the longest he's said so far, it must have been a lot worth to him to let me know. It took him over an hour to eat and, although his eyes longed to finish it off, he pushed the plates back and wiped his mouth. He asked, "Can I go to bed now, Arden?"

I nodded agreeingly. "Of course; I'll stick around, if you need anything." Then I added, "When I came out of a Russian prison shortly after the war, I was pretty near in your shape then, too. I remember very vividly that I could not sleep in a bed, it was too soft; so I simply laid down on the mat beside it and covered myself with a blanket. It did the trick." I grinned.

He grinned back and immediately fell asleep, just like that. I stood vigilant over my young friend and watched every move of his, comforting him with my love. When dusk showed itself through the window, Willy became restless and finally opened his eyes with some painful expression. But his look mellowed as soon as he saw me.

I said, "You had a good sleep, Willy, feel like anything?"

He stretched himself first and thought for a while. "If I could eat some more ... I'm still hungry."

"But, of course," I supported his suggestion. "I can get some right now, unless you would like to go out? The restaurant in this hotel is not too ... vegetarian, if I may call it that. It's best to stay off meat for a while, Willy."

His answer surprised me, "I want to become a vegetarian, too, Arden; I don't care much for meat and the rest anyway." Then he said, "If I could stay in the room, my legs are not too strong."

"Today is Sunday, tomorrow I shall find a place where they can make a drink to my specifications," I suggested, "that'll give you more strength again."

Passing by a drugstore gave me an idea and I entered. In the baby food section I found soya milk and bought several cans. This liquid is a complete food and might do him more good than anything solid. Coming back into the room loaded with bags of foodstuff, my young friend had turned on the TV, but switched it off again. I said, "I don't mind if you watch."

But he waved at the tube as if to say that he wasn't interested. So I lined up all the goodies on the table. He really liked the taste of the soya milk and slowly emptied one can. "I feel full already," he remarked, but added a vegetable salad anyway.

In the middle of the night, around two o'clock, Willy began to move as if in distress. I knew that he was pestered by a bad dream and woke him up to give him assurance of his safety in my presence. Relieved, he took my hand and fell asleep again.

First thing in the morning I phoned the Bonsons to give them the good news. Willy was too shy to say anything, but on the other end of the line the revelation produced great joy and Marg said under crying, "Give him a big hug for me, Arden."

During the morning we saw a doctor who practiced

113

orthomolecular medicine and nutrition, and he was just what we needed. He took a blood sample of my young friend to find out whether there was something drastically wrong with him and also to establish all his allergies. Willy was clearly undernourished and his intestine loaded with worms and the like. Otherwise he couldn't find much wrong and said, while writing the prescription, "Besides good food he needs the whole line of vitamins and minerals. Well, you have assured me that you know the subject thoroughly, Mister Hellmer. I trust you to go about it slowly; patience is the key to the young man's full health again. A lot of rest is a <u>must</u>, combined with the observance of his allergies in the beginning. His allergy list will be here this afternoon and my secretary will have it ready for you."

When we drove around town to see some of the famous spectacles, Willy suddenly said, "You think I can have a cigarette?"

I smiled at him sidewards and answered, "But of course, Willy, I'll buy a pack."

"No, just one, don't buy the whole pack," he said rather quickly.

Out of the car and overlooking the bay, he satisfied his craving by inhaling deeply. However, he flipped the cigarette away only half-smoked. He tried to explain it several times, but gave up finally.

During our flight back home, Willy asked me to tell him about the war, my imprisonment and the times later on. As I went along with my story -- reluctantly, I must say -- speaking about the killings, the dead and my struggles to cope with the world after the war I didn't know much about, omitting my marriage, he seemed to show satisfaction. Perhaps he thought that I surely must understand him, having gone through that kind of experience, which I did up to a certain extent. But the past had taught me also, that never any two circumstances are alike.

While my young friend waited for the luggage at the pick-up, I quickly stepped to the telephone to give the Bonsons a ring. I suggested to Marg that we drive past their place to get acquainted slowly first. I said, "I think Willy is rather shy and embarrassed to see you, believe it or not. Maybe we should let Hanna come to my place first after school. You see what I mean?"

"Yes, yes, good idea, Arden," she answered in thought, "he has to get to know us again all over on his time. How is he?"

So I told her quickly about the doctor's findings, but that his spirits still were in good shape.

Driving past the Bonson farm without stopping was appreciated by my companion, he only had a quick look past me in the direction of the house. However, at my farm entrance he became alive and his eyes wandered around to take it all in. I simply said, "This is your home now, Willy."

He stepped into the house ahead of me, as if he had thought about this moment often. In his room he went straight to the box I had made for the children several years before for their weekly earnings to be stored. He opened it and saw a stack of dollar bills in it -- I had added every month a bit. His eyes looked quickly at me, only to see tears running down my cheeks again.

Without unpacking, we walked first to the garden, the chickens and the workshop. His heart must've jumped when he saw the Windjammer and Venturer beside each other. He grabbed my hand and called out: "Two of them!"

I remember faintly that I had discussed my dreams of flying again early with the children. I explained this and that Hanna was the last to fly next year. "And you, of course, young man," I added. I could see his imagination going to work. Then he looked down at his body and said with raised shoulders, "I guess I have a lot to work on my weight and strength."

Putting an arm around him, I laughed, "The worst is behind you, Willy. We don't worry about peanuts."

Suddenly he threw his arms around me and cried and cried. He certainly needed that. With arms around our backs, we walked toward the house. Now I could feel his determination to face what comes, he was ready!

Chapter 16
And There IS Love

When Willy and I had settled in and it was going on four o'clock, I suggested to him, "Soon Hanna will come home from school; why don't you wait on top of the hill from where you can overlook the road right up to their house. She's bound to come up here as soon as she's dropped her books at the house."

He nodded, surprised, and left immediately, an indication that he must look forward to their first meeting again, which might seem an infinity to him since last time. I would've liked to be present, but knew very well that two young hearts have their own special ways when it comes to moments like that.

In order to still my mind, I began to prepare the evening meal. I wanted to put a lot of planning into Willy's food intake; he needed the best to get on his feet again. While in the basement, I heard their voices outside. Looking through a crack in the door, I saw the two walking slowly beside each other toward the pond. It was not their old free-spirited and happy relationship, I could see that. A lot had to be renewed and to be healed. But I wasn't worried; we old ones can learn from the young in that category.

Looking out of the kitchen window a bit later, I saw them in the boat, rowing around the water and even heard their laughter. Well, well, we can't have enough of that; it also added to my happiness.

After I had phoned Marg to tell her that things were picking up and that Hanna probably would like to stay for supper, I went outside and hammered with a large spoon on a pot and called to my young friends: "Come and get it, supper is ready!"

They came out of the workshop, but only Hanna ran toward

me with a laugh, "Hi, Arden, can I eat here?" I held out a hand with an inviting gesture.

She looked around for Willy and wondered that he wasn't right behind her. I whispered to her, "Willy is not too steady on his legs yet, he can't run. We got to take it easy with him for a while."

"I see," she whispered back, "okay, Arden."

We three together again at the table, it truly was an event I never will forget. There wasn't much talk, but a lot of smiles went back and forth between us.

Hanna was reluctant to leave, so I said, "It's dark already, girl, come back tomorrow. How about your homework, if there is any?"

"Oh, I forgot all about it," she called out, "I better get going then. See you tomorrow after school." And out she ran.

"I will be so old already," my young friend began later on in the living room, "to go back to high school. You think they..."

"Nothing to worry about, Willy," I comforted him. "Only a week and a half ago I read that even much older people go back to make their high school diploma because they need it to find proper work. There are plenty now, even married couples." A few moments later I added, "As long as you want it, that's the important part."

"I want it, Arden," he said very determined. "I need it for an engineer, that's what I want to become, an engineer."

With a smile I patted him on the arm and said, "You sure get my support all the way."

However, I detected some reluctance in him; was at a loss, though, what it might be, until a week later when I found out why.

* * *

Then he approached me with the words, "You know, Arden, I could go out and make money first, that way I can pay for high school and college."

It was in the workshop and I had to sit down first, so as not to come up with a hasty answer. That's what was on his mind all the time, I had detected something he was working on.

I finally decided to put everything on the table and to be frank and forward. I said, "You know, Willy, I had planned on adopting you as my son. Does it make any difference to you whether I'm your blood father? I always wanted a son and ever since I met you

117

first and got to know you, I said to myself that if I would have had a son, he should've been like you, Willy." I paused for a moment.

His face was expressionless, so I asked him, "If you don't mind having me as a father?"

"Sure, Arden," he said, not looking up, "but I mean, is it that simple?"

I got up and walked toward him, holding out my hand. He got up, too, and took it. Next we put our arms around each other again and I said with all the warmth, "I love you, son." We both had tears running down our cheeks.

To my amazement and joy he asked a few minutes later, "You think I can adopt your name, too?"

"Oh, Willy," I called out, "there's nobody else I'd rather give my name." Then I added with a deep grin, "And pay for his education ... the best."

* * *

However, first back to the present. I wanted Willy to be able to look after himself, food-wise, and so I began to teach him the fundamentals of nutrition. I had a lot of books on the subject and chose for him only some selected ones, those important to him.

The very first thing in the morning we made a nutritional drink for breakfast. All the goodies went into it, like grapes, ground-up nuts, a half an apple, pre-done carrot juice and his vitamins and minerals; they all were mixed and liquefied in a blender. On other mornings we used papaya, mangoes or pears, whatever was available. That was all for him until lunch. "Spoon it slowly like soup," I advised him. Banana, cherries and blueberries became his favorites.

Unfortunately, he had to stay off yogurt and brewer's yeast (both very nutritious foods) for a while because of his allergy to them.

On the third day I heard him early already in the kitchen before six, making some carrot juice with the extractor. I was awake and joined him with a smile.

He greeted me with the words, "I feel so good, Arden, you think I should have this drink three times a day? Every time I have it in the morning, I feel the strength afterward, I just _feel_ it."

"It might be an idea," I thought it over for a while. "But I suggest to add more fiber at noon and at night, something not cut

118

too fine with the blender. Then have one meal only fruits and the other only vegetables."

I had gone into the living room to get a hook and came back with it. "Here, read this later. It's about the famous Muesli Diet, by Doctor Bircher-Benner, a Swiss physician who got many people back to health, given up as incurable. The doctor who runs the clinic today emphasizes at times to eat this diet three times a day with good results. You might find beneficial pointers in that book. I correspond with him, by the way, a very open-minded man."

Late Friday afternoon, Hanna phoned to let me know that she would have her supper at home because of a lot of homework. She finally arrived at eight and said, "We've a new teacher and he believes in doing <u>much</u> work at home."

I laughed and said, "Good for you, girl, many kids leave school today and hardly can read. Look, as a boy I had so much homework all the time that I never got around to playing except on Sundays. I remember from my daughters that I was way ahead of them in knowledge, in comparison with their particular grade. You're just spoiled in this country."

On Saturday morning we walked down to the Bonsons' Willy was ready now to face them again. He still seemed shy, though, when he entered the house, but everything was all right after Marg had put her arms around him for a big welcome.

I kind of had to laugh about Bill, who gave Willy a big bang on the back with his flat hand and said, grinning, "Now we'll be neighbors all the time, Willy."

In the afternoon some flights were put in, but the conditions were not too good anymore with fall approaching. What we needed for long and comfortable flights were cumulus clouds. However, Willy enjoyed himself in just watching them running into the wind, swinging their feet onto the pedals to get the propeller rotating and stay up in the air, then rise slowly.

The Bonson parents and I were sitting together on garden chairs, watching and having a chat away from the crowd. In an asking way, kind of, Marg said, "Does he know already that you're going to adopt him? I mean, did you discuss it or does he just presume that he is with you now for good?"

I had to laugh and said with a twinkle in my eyes, "Yes, Marg, it's all settled. As sensitive he was at first, now he even wants my

119

name with the adoption, and get rid of the past once and for all. Kids have a way to cope with things in their owns minds."

"We had a call from the social worker a week ago," Marg continued, "whether we had heard anything from Willy. Some of his relatives want to know. Apparently there is an inheritance waiting. Well, something about an inheritance anyway. Perhaps you want to investigate? It might be important."

I nodded and said in thought, "It might, it might; I'll give her a ring next week and see what it is all about. Besides, I want to start the adoption proceedings soon and have to see her anyway. Thanks for bringing it up. I'll talk to the boy first thing on Monday."

On Wednesday, Willy and I drove into town to speak with the social worker, having given her a ring first for an appointment. The young man was kind of nervous about it; he seemed to have a dislike for anything official or anybody sitting in an office. But I was determined to straighten it all out; I wasn't about to let things hang in the air, it was not my way of doing business.

"We had several calls already from a lawyer who represents the young man's relatives from his deceased father's side," she began. "Apparently there is an inheritance waiting and Willy is the first in line. After a waiting period of a certain time, the money, if that's what it is, falls to the other relatives."

I looked at my new son to get his reaction on the matter at hand and have his say, but he just raised his shoulders. So I asked the lady, "Can I have a few minutes in private with him, we'd like to talk this over on our own?"

"Sure, there is an empty room," she said, pointing to a door.

On our own I asked, "What do you say, Willy?"

He just raised his shoulders again. So I continued with a suggestion. "Look, Willy, we don't need the money. Eventually, you'll inherit everything from me anyway and that'll be a lot. Perhaps they need it more than we do now. But, I don't want to talk you into it."

In thought and shaking his head, he said, "My father never thought about me. He beat me and abused me and all that. Now I want something from him."

I couldn't see into the young man's mind and heart, but tried to understand his feelings. I said, "You think you should proceed then and accept it?"

120

He simply nodded with an expressionless face.

After the social worker had given us the address of the lawyer, I asked, "I intend to adopt Willy as my son, where can we go? It should be simple enough, shouldn't it be?"

"I'm sure glad to hear that, Mister Hellmer. I was wondering already what we should do with the young man now," the lady said happily. "That solves many of our problems here and we can close the book on this case."

Then she added in a questioning manner, "Aren't you the gentleman all the papers wrote so much about? I think it was a year or two ago."

I nodded, grinning.

"Oh, I'm so glad to meet you personally," she said, obviously very delighted."You see, my husband is an airline pilot and we all rooted for you. That press was just awful," she shook her head, "those people are shameless."

And so she went on, warming up that half-forgotten story again for Willy and me. But we sat and listened.

After having filled out and signed the adoption papers later on, we drove to the lawyer, an elderly gentleman. There was quite a sum at stake, namely eighty thousand dollars. I glanced at my young friend, my son that is, and noticed a grin of satisfaction. However, he had to be eighteen years of age to receive his inheritance, and that was still two years hence. I also told the attorney about our adoption and Willy's change of surname to mine.

In the car on our way home, Willy was quiet until we drove through the farm gate, where he simply said, "I could give it to somebody." That's all. I knew what he meant, of course.

Now I had a son and Willy a father and we two were growing and flowering in our new roles. Although never spoken about nor physically demonstrated, our love was pure and our hearts and Souls embraced often for that ultimate inner feeling.

Chapter 17
A Goat Named Jodie

My life began to change slowly since I had a son. There were so many things Willy needed now, and the ideas he came up with, that we often planned together, although I encouraged him to be creative and think problems through himself. Often enough, though, I found it too hard to simply stand back.

Willy got me really involved in nutrition, foods and gardening again, because now he wanted to know it all in detail and there were dozens of questions. Sure, I know, I simply should've given him a book or two and follow my next project in the workshop, industriously. But I didn't. Well, he was my son and I wanted him to know it all first-hand out of my years of investigations and experiences. After all, it took me a lot of reading and many books to come to my present level of understanding.

Slowly my son made his way back into life and became more talkative, not that he ever had been particularly chatty at any time before, like Hanna, for instance. In any case, I was able to pick up a few pieces here and there out of his past couple of years of 'adventure on the run', so to speak. It surprised me that he survived it so well, mentally and emotionally as he did. To me it was proof of a very strong character in the young man.

One day Willy approached me with the words, "You know, Arden, we've so much grass growing wild, couldn't we have a goat? In some of the books, they say that goats' milk and cheese is much better and that even allergic people can digest it," He looked at me as if to say, 'Come on, let's get one.'

"That'll be a lot of work," I answered. "Who's going to milk it? Fences have to be built. And cheese making takes its time."

Well, we got a goat all right, after having consulted the Bonsons about it first. After all, they were the farmers with a lot of experience. Bill was telling us that goats were a cinch, compared with cows, although he never had had one himself.

With their advice still ringing in our ears, we finally found a milk-giving goat not too far away and brought it home. Her name was Jodie and our liking for each other was instant. "You don't need any fencing," Bill had been telling us, "just hammer a metal spike into the ground, fasten a rope to it and to the animal's neck, and you're all set. When it has eaten all the grass in that circle, simple move it. One of us can show you how to milk."

Helen was the one most helpful and by Christmas we had our steady daily milk supply and, particularly I, was glad that it worked out so easily.

To make cheese, we added a Finnish culture, called Piima to the raw milk -- years before I had sent for and experimented with Piima until I found that I was allergic to dairy products. Unlike yogurt, where one had to destroy the enzymes in the raw milk first by heating it to at least 165 degrees Fahrenheit, this culture could be added forthwith. When the goat's milk had reached the consistency of clabber milk, we put it into cheesecloth to drain the water and let it hang until it had solidified. That was our homemade cheese and it even agreed with me, if I ate it sparingly.

In January Willy had put on enough weight and reached his old strength again to be ready to go back to school. He had done a lot of homework, assisted by Hanna, to get back into a good mental state. In any case, he himself said that he was ready to face the school world again. I had noticed that he worked himself up to the first encounter with some of his old buddies and friends, all now three classes ahead of him. My son had done a lot of maturing in many ways, perhaps more so than his peers.

When he came home after the first school day, he grinned and said, "It was all right, Arden, they found out quickly enough that I wasn't a push-over. There was only one of the old teachers left, Mrs. Audrey, and I always had liked her. The girls were okay, they know that Hanna and I are friends. I just laughed at the boys and they stopped teasing me after a while. Their attitude doesn't bother me."

I don't know what exactly happened, of course, but can imagine it. I was glad that he withstood his first encounter in school again so well. It also meant a lot to me; I thought that Willy had suffered enough. Now I could put my mind back to technical work, which I had been missing, kind of. From bachelorhood to fatherhood in a short time, it had a lot to do with compromise on my old life.

After Helen was finished with the milking one morning, I brought Jodie, our goat, out to the pasture behind the hill, from where we made our flights. Surprised, I saw her wandering around again freely a half an hour later, dragging the rope with the metal spike behind. So I went out once more to tie her down, and this time I pushed the spike up to the loop in the ground.

However, Jodie was free again not too long hence and I thought that somebody might be playing a joke on me. Having secured her again, I walked back only to turn around to look over the crest of the hill to see who the culprit was. It was Jodie herself! As soon as I was out of sight, she simply put one of her horns through the loop of the spike, to slowly work it out of the ground. I had to laugh so hard that tears ran down my cheeks. We were the owners of a very smart goat and I liked her twice as much for that.

Jodie had gotten loose before and our flowers had made their way into her stomach; obviously, she liked the good food. So I tightened her to a door of one of the outbuildings, while talking to her to smarten up, until we would come up with a spike she was not able to work out of the ground. By noon, though, she had tangled herself around all kinds of old stuff on the ground, so that I had to go out and tighten her to a tree this time. That loving animal simply took too much of my attention.

Willy and Hanna began to jog every day to get themselves into good shape for their first flight in May or June. Since Hanna's artificial foot did not quite sit and work right while running, a new one had to be designed and built, suitable for a higher pressure on her leg stump.

The two youngsters did the job all by themselves, with not even one of my suggestions. Hanna also carried her new foot to school so that she could participate in sports there, too. I was so glad that I had introduced them all along the line to my technical know-how and concepts, it sure helped them now to be very self-sufficient.

Of course, we all had had a laugh about our smart goat. One evening after supper Willy approached me with the words, "Jodie is slowly running dry, Arden. It would be a good idea to get a second goat, who will be giving milk during Jodie's off-season.

That way we always have enough milk and can continue making our cheese."

I waited with my answer for a while, although I knew what to answer, namely that I would refuse his request. I finally said, "We will have cheese for quite some time, Willy, and the milk is not all that important to either of us. To look after two goats is quite a job and, to be honest, it takes too much of my time away from what I really want to do in the workshop."

Deep down I had suspected it and now could see his disagreement coming and went on, "You are in school, son, and who does the milking and other chores often? Helen." I shook my head in saying, "If we start something, we should continue it on our own and not depend on others, no matter how friendly and close we are with each other."

"But, dad," he injected quickly, "Helen does it because she likes it and not because we are not doing it. And a second goat doesn't make all that much difference."

I looked deeply into his eyes and said, "It does to me, Willy. There is a fine line of ethics I believe in and like to adhere to. Helen might like the job, but just the same it's ours. And, perhaps, I should talk to her, not to let things get out of hand, in a way. I'm not cross with her; often, though, there is a lot to do on their own farm where she might be needed. No, young man, a second goat will not do, it's over our heads, as far as I'm concerned. Proportionally things have to be right and make sense, and that goes for the animal also. I don't believe in just having an animal for only my benefit. And two of them? We simply cannot look after them properly."

I saw anger manifesting in my son and countered it with love as much as I could. It was so hard to keep one's own temper; often anger begets anger. What else could I only have said? Unfortunately, his channel of good reasoning was closed. Our first serious disagreement and it had to turn out like that.

In any case, he got up and walked into his room without another word or even a good-night. I was completely relaxed, but very sad. We parted on a negative footing and it left a bitter taste.

For the rest of the evening I watched TV, not that I was able to dislodge my thoughts and feelings from the foregoing completely. If he only would come out of his room and say something, but he didn't.

125

In the morning during our breakfast chores in the kitchen only a few words were spoken between us. I had decided not to take any farther initiative; after all, he was old enough to either recognize a lesson to be learned or brood over the subject for a while. He had to bring his anger under control, a matter I knew only too well because it had almost cost me my life. There might have been other words, more soothing perhaps, I should've used, but I wasn't perfect either and experience was not on my side.

When Willy came home from school, he walked straight into the workshop, sat down in one of the easy chairs and said, "Can I talk to you, dad?"

I had a good inner feeling and looked at him in my old and easy way, smiling. "But of course, Willy. I'm here for you."

"That's not what I meant ..." he answered embarrassed, not looking at me. "I was wrong last night, Arden." He used my first name at times when it was important.

I sat down, too, and looked at him with encouragement. He continued. "I don't know why I got so mad at you and now I don't understand it anymore. Now I'm angry at myself. It was not right, it sure wasn't."

I got up and held out my hand with a grin and he took it, very relieved, only to throw his arms around me. And so we stood for a while, feeling our hearts.

When we parted he suggested, "Maybe we should get rid of Jodie, too. I'm hardly here anymore when she has to be milked."

"No, my boy," I shook my head in saying, "I like Jodie too much now and she is part of our life. Don't you feel the same?" He nodded happily. I continued, "We let her get dry and just keep her as our pet. Maybe we can teach her some manners, not to eat our flowers. No, I could not imagine selling her to a stranger. She never would forgive us." I grinned at him.

Walking to the house to make supper, Willy hooked into my arm and said, "I can learn so much from you, dad; I was so foolish last night, so dumb." I simply patted his hand, joyous that it turned out that way.

While preparing the food together, I suggested, "There's bound to be disagreements between us, son; after all, we're not living in heaven here." I grinned at him. "There is one thing you never should do again, though, go to bed with your anger. It's one of the poorest practices I can think of. Anger is like a vice on your

126

heart, but only recognition, your own awareness, can open up that vice. I know, it's easy to say now, but one can nurse and nurture the opposite of anger, like forgiveness and tolerance, and learn to embrace them beforehand. Then, next time, one is well prepared and takes the initiative. Have you got an idea why I know it so well?"

He shook his head, but suggested, "Because you were angry at one time?"

I chuckled and said, "Yes, more than once, Willy. Often anger ran my life and blinded me to good relationships with my fellow men. My marriage break-up I can partly blame on that. And at my last anger bout, if I want to call it that, I almost lost my life, and you and Hanna were there, too. Remember when a certain violent and angry man kicked in my teeth?" I kept on nodding and nodding. "Yes, you see, he picked up my state of mind and was not to let me dominate him. It was my anger."

"How do you know all this, Dad?" Willy asked surprised. "I mean, did you figure all this out by yourself?"

"Dreams, Willy, I learn from my dreams and those experiences," I replied with joy that he followed it up with a question. "There are also dream Masters, highly spiritual beings, who help and assist. One can meet them, more often hear them speak."

"Maybe I should start my dream journal again," he suggested, "is is still there?" I nodded with a smile.

During mealtime our vibrations were back to normal again; obviously, a lot of learning had to be done on both sides. Although we did not speak while doing the dishes, there was an inner communication on the level of Soul.

In the living room later on, I said, "I know you went through a lot with all the other young people on the run, so to speak, and that kind of environment always seems to breed the negative passions more than anything else. You see, Willy, I was in a similar position as a soldier, having to kill, being brutal and violent in the name of an idea or ideal for my country. Sure, it's supposed to be all legal, but it sure isn't legal to your subconscious mind. This is a very vast subject I'm just beginning to understand now, often assisted through my dreams and dream Friends."

"I hardly dream anymore, dad," Willy said. "Maybe they will start again when I write them down."

"I'm almost certain of that," I answered.

"Mind telling me more about the war, dad?" my son asked.

Suddenly I became very serious and in shaking my head, I said, "I <u>do</u> mind! No, son, I doubt whether I ever will. I try to heal my old wounds, and since I can't bury them, I keep them tucked away. Some people have to dig our their old experiences again and again, and even write books about them. They have to tell the rest of the world to find their equilibrium again. Others have to employ a psychiatrist to find their track back into life and society. I belong to neither one." Then, "If you think it might help to speak of your experience, we ..."

He cut me off in vigorously shaking his head. Then he said, very determined, "I'm <u>all right</u>, dad." I did not pursue it.

This serious talk in the living room that evening made a completely new boy out of my son in many ways. Now he stood with both feet on the ground – probably for the very first time in his young life – I think I had become his good example and role model. If I, as a much older person, was able to let go of the past and even make it a point to work on the positive aspects of life, so could he. And he did!

Doing some deep thinking about the foregoing, though, made me grin to myself. It was a beast rather, that started Willy off on his new road to awareness and understanding – it was Jodie, our goat.

Chapter 18
Graduation of Beast, Pilots and Students

When I watched Jodie walking with me on the leash, I thought I detected some pride, now that she had advanced from a milk-producing goat to a family pet. She definitely recognized her new status and, as I saw it, that put her above a simple animal mentality. I was usually the one who took her out on my daily walks and she appreciated the change from her secure but limited thirty-yard line in the field, from where there was no escape anymore, since I had made a spike she could not work out of the ground.

I always talked to her, pointing out things and trying to tell her that she actually could run around free if she only would behave and not eat our nice flowers, garden vegetables and other things not suitable for the stomach of a goat. Every time we came past one of our flower boxes, I let her smell the plants and called out: "No, no, no," and pulled on the leash. Then I pointed to the many dandelions in the grass and said, nodding, "Yes, yes, Jodie, you can have them."

And so I tried to educate our animal friend; doubted, however, that she would adhere to my schooling. But the surprise was on me! After doing this for over two months, I thought that it wouldn't do much harm now to test her and give it a try and see, not having my hopes too high. I let her loose, but made sure she didn't get out of my sight.

I watched her for three days in a row, neglecting what I was doing in the workshop. Not once did she try to eat anything forbidden, not even when I was hidden from her sight. Well, well, she had some higher intelligence after all, something I rather had doubted. It was a graduation for Jodie into a higher consciousness.

So we let her run around, as one would do with a dog, having an occasional eye on her. Only during the nights was she locked into her roomy stable, an old machine shed.

Sometimes we saw our pet goat wandering long distances over the fields into the woods and I was thinking about bear. Would she recognize them as her enemies? The instinct probably would tell her.

* * *

The time had arrived for Hanna and Willy to have their first flights. It was a Sunday noon, with some cumulus clouds already above, a necessity for our young flyers to stay aloft, longer than the muscle power would permit.

Willy was first, and with a last look in my direction he ran down the hill. My next awareness was Jodie running alongside the glider and even overtaking it. When the young pilot swung his legs inside to get the propeller going, the puzzled goat tried to jump up at my son several times. It couldn't follow the climbing plane into the air, of course. I simply had to laugh with all the others, the way it stood on its hind legs, looking up, running another twenty yards and looking up again on its hind legs, as if yearning to be with its human friend up there. It looked so comical.

With the goat's performance we almost had forgotten about Willy, but he was doing well and turning back to fly overhead. We waved and called up to him, while he wiggled the wings with joy. In only fifteen minutes he was able to catch an updraft and not too long after that we saw him circling under a cumulus cloud.

I finally put my attention back on the ground again and particularly to Jodie. How in the world was she able to get loose? I called her to me and examined her collar; she had chewed through the rope. Her desire for freedom must have been very strong. How could I be mad at and scold her. She simply did not understand why we wanted to tie her down because she thought herself to be part of the family and the crowd, which also meant, of course, to participate in all our activities.

I was glad that the wind had picked up a bit, since Hanna was next with the Venturer and she could do better with a good wind in her favor. How would she make out with her artificial foot, I wondered? Perhaps I worried too much, because she had no trouble whatsoever getting into the air. Oh, I was so happy for her! Now we all could fly like birds and talk shop about our experiences together, with the exception of Marg Bonson, who didn't mind at all, and Jodie, of course, who didn't know better (?) and enjoyed her freedom more than anything else.

Wisely, we had dressed our two new glider pilots warm enough and saw them now circling high below the cumulus for hours, often seen together, enjoying their company during their flight, too. When in the late afternoon the clouds seem to develop into dark, black thunder heads and some faint rumbling reached our ears, the two youngsters must have seen and heard it also, because early enough they had decided to get out of what might be called a dangerous situation. I was glad that they had the sense to come back at once; after all, I had included just such a possibility into their training curriculum.

We on the ground were ready to assist them and hold the planes by the wing tips, after they had landed. Hanna was first and did not land with her legs, but rather preferred a landing on the sled-like skids. I couldn't blame her, because after over three hours in the air the handicapped leg stump must have felt lame. However, Willy did no such thing and landed perfectly with his legs. I guess pride might have played a part in that.

We hardly had moved the two gliders into the workshop and the rain drummed down in buckets on the metal roof. Wow, that was close! I had to have another talk with the youngsters; they had had no experience to cope with that kind of weather in the air. Well, did I? No, but I had much more flying experience and never would dare to tackle a thunderstorm. I did once during the war in Germany, but my glider plane was of a more solid structure and build, and capable of higher speeds. It could withstand storm-like winds. In fact, some of us flew then with the assistance of a thunderstorm over the country for hundreds of miles to break records.

We had found enough plastic sheeting to put over our heads and dash for the house, where we had a little party to celebrate the graduation of two new glider pilots. It was a joyous atmosphere with a lot of laughter. Mixing juices in the kitchen, I suddenly felt an arm around me from the back and a voice whispered into my ear, "Thanks, Arden." It was Hanna and she also gave me a kiss on the cheek. Her deep smile said the rest.

To my surprise, Willy had a little speech for the occasion and said, "Hanna and I want to give special thanks to Arden, who never tired of teaching us to fly with the Windjammer and the

131

Venturer, if only on the ground. His experience taught us a lot and you saw the end result today, we stayed up all that time. I was thinking about you a lot up there, Dad." For a moment his voice faltered and he had to swallow hard. He finished with the words, "Thanks, Dad, thanks for everything." He put his arms around me for a squeeze. Then he said, "I, we, Hanna and me, wanted to say actually more; we worked together on the speech, but I forgot the other words." He raised his hands and shoulders. Everybody applauded and gave their approval to make the young man feel better.

I was thinking about our pirate times together, some two hundred or so years before. What different lives we lived today in other bodies and positions. All of us had been together in that reincarnation and all of us are together again here and now. Would we ever be able to discuss our past? I had to grin when my thoughts came back to the present.

Everybody was looking at me so I got up and said, "I could hold a long, long speech, but I won't. You give me too much credit, you guys; we're all in this together and I'm not that special. I just happened to be at the right place at the right time to find such nice and understanding neighbors and even a son," I looked with a grin at Willy. "You and I already know enough about spiritual matters, however, to understand that in God's plan nothing is ever luck or simply happens by chance; instead, it was predetermined by our Creator." I gave them a half-knowing and secret grin. "And on that note I shall sit down again and keep my lips closed."

An hour or so later, Marg and Bill joined me on the sofa. All the young people had gone into the kitchen to make supper. The rain still was coming down outside and nobody would dare and walk back to the Bonson farm in that pour. I could've driven them, of course, but our happy vibrations kept us together for an evening meal. In any case, there was enough for all to eat and nobody minded the vegetarian fare.

Marg, beside me, began with, "Did I detect something in your speech? Something you know and we don't, Arden?" She laughed.

"Oh, you guys," I laughed back at them, "did I sound like that? Well," I became more serious, "we all have been together before, I know that already. At one time you two had been my parents, believe it or not. But, I don't think I'm at liberty to expose some of our past lives. Whatever turns me on and gives me those

132

dream experiences -- I call them dream Masters -- will also give you the experiences and knowledge when your time is ripe. It's not for me to say, Marg and Bill, although I'm tempted often enough, being so close to you all. To keep quiet is probably my biggest test and lesson."

Into their thinking I said once more, "What I just passed on to you is among us three, okay?"

"But, of course, Arden, we never would say anything without your permission," Marg assured me with a hand squeeze on my arm.

Then Bill said, "Maybe we're not putting enough attention on all this spiritual stuff, I hardly dream anymore. Well, the farm work, you know, we're just too busy."

Then Marg added, "There is a lot on our minds right now with the big loan we took. This fall we will be in a better position and can relax more. Helen sure is a big help; without her income and contribution we really would be struggling."

I just nodded and wished that I could be of more help financially, but didn't dare to open my mouth in that respect, knowing Bill only two well; he wouldn't like my offer. How could I blame him – would I in his position?

* * *

A week later was holiday and graduation time for the kids. Willy came home from school and called out: "I passed two classes, Arden. Here, look at my report card and a letter from the principal."

I shook my head with delight and read the letter with a deep grin. I said, "I knew you could do it, son, your hard work paid off. Oh, I'm so glad!"

"Next year I'll do it again," he laughed, "and graduate high school with the others together, you'll see."

"I believe you," I said and put my arms around him. "You know, I'm proud that you could stay out of the workshop; although the temptation was there often enough, at this time school is more consequential. And now you even fly, what can be more important at the moment?" His happy eyes met mine without another word.

A half an hour later, Hanna came running into the workshop, where we two had walked, breathing hard. She said, "Isn't it a dandy, Arden, that Willy jumped a class?"

I nodded, grinning, and accepted her squeeze with delight and satisfaction. I asked, "When are you two leaving for your mountain hike and climb with Mister Bushell? On Monday, isn't it?"

"Yes," they both said. "On Sunday afternoon we have to put things together," Hanna added, "because Monday early we're leaving from school. The teacher's wife also comes, that makes us all together sixteen. It'll be so much fun and for a whole week!"

While the two were on their mountain tour for a week or so, I decided to go down to the Bonsons and help them with the farming. I could use the change and felt like hard labor as a physical workout; besides, they needed the help right now. First, Bill wanted to argue with me, but I simply cut him off with, "Either you accept me as a field worker or I'm not speaking to you anymore." I said that with a grin, but he grasped the seriousness behind my words.

After a couple of days, he told me early upon my arrival, "I'll be damned if I understood you at first, Arden, but I think I do now."

I gave him a nod and a good slap on the back, an understanding between us two without words. We both parted with knowing grins.

Chapter 19
Children of Hard Labor

After having worked in the fields of the Bonson farm all day with only a sandwich for lunch, I accepted Marg's invitation for supper. She said, "I know you like to go home and have your vegetarian fare, but today I've lots of it on the table here, too. Come on and stay, that way you can relax a little. Aren't you overdoing it a bit? I mean, you're not as used to that kind of work as our men are."

This was my sixth day of farm work and I began to like it. Although my body was not of a heavy build, I needed a change, a different physical perspective. Besides, I wanted to help my neighbors in their hard times, knowing very well that they wouldn't hire anybody to save money. Anyway, I thought that I had become too soft for my own good.

"Well, Marg, if I'm overdoing it, it's sent from heaven," I laughed, in answering her, "because I'm beginning to feel much better. Sometimes one loses sight of his physical good."

Having washed up and just taken a seat at the table, Bill, Helen and the boys came and my neighbor said with a laugh, "So Marg was able to talk you into it, hey? I hoped you would stay, we hardly get to talk anymore; you're just working too hard, old boy."

I simply answered with a grin, looking forward to a little chat myself.

There was plenty on the table and I even indulged in a piece of chicken. When I saw the quantity of food they consumed, I was not surprised anymore of the men's build and strength; their frames needed it.

In their living room later on, I said, "I had a lot of time to do some thinking, away from what I'm usually doing. Children of hard labor, you might call it. So, here is one suggestion, if you want to hear it, that is?"

Bill said, "Come on now, Arden, you know we don't mind to listen to a smart fellow."

"Yes, yes," I grinned, "I also have often impression that I talk you into things and you wind up with a lot of hardship, like right now. Remember, I was the one who started you off on organic farming."

They all objected vigorously and Bill said rather too seriously, "Come, come now, Arden, you're not fair to yourself nor to us. We wanted it! You just helped with ... well, with the magazine you gave us to read and in passing on your knowledge. You got to give us credit for some initiative, too."

I did it again, I thought; I stepped into a wasp nest with my big mouth, so I said, to calm things down, "I know myself only too well and have the tendency in talking people into. my way of thinking. I'm glad to hear you didn't see it that way and I apologize if I said the wrong thing."

"No need for that, Arden," Marg said, looking at me and then at Bill, "sometimes we would be better off, too, in choosing finer words and answers." Her eyes were glued to her husband, indicating that she meant him. Then she said to me, "You had a suggestion, Arden, some child of hard labor," she grinned.

I grinned back at her and began, "I guess it's a farmer's lot that everything comes in at once, or goes wrong together, like the weather, for instance. Nothing in your occupation is ever slowly tapered and your control is very limited. I always wanted to ask whether you can sell all your produce when it's ready? It's such a short time to get rid of that quantity."

"That's a farmer's life all right," Bill called out.

"I kind of have an idea to be better prepared for that particular time of plenty," I said, "especially now, where you are one of the few to sell only organic produce. Go into a big market or a speciality store and look at their prices for organic vegetables. But why? There is enough here. You could serve several big stores in Vancouver. They might be taking advantage of you and putting up prices when it isn't necessary."

"Good point," I heard Bill, "good point."

"I would pull the rug from underneath them," I continued,

"and advertise. Not just a little ad in the paper, but a big one, with your particular heading. Something like: Bonson's Organic Produce. And then list below the vegetables available at the moment. At the end put your address, telephone number and also, Retailers Invited. Here, I'll make you a drawing," and I drew on a piece of paper Marg had given me.

"Put the ad in both of the big papers twice a week," I suggested, "so people and retailers know when and what to expect. I bet before you have to pay for the ads, you'll already have the cash back from the sold produce. Did you ever see the Dutch here in town selling their flowers and the other stuff? They brought this method back from Holland, and it works here, too. Speed is the key to your success. Anything deteriorating as quickly as produce needs a special consideration and the one with the best idea will be the winner."

Their minds worked on what I had said. I continued in the same vein. "I happen to know an advertising agent who worked for me at one time. I can go to him and ask his advice how your ad exactly should be done. If you wish, I can consult him. He does it for nothing; to him it's just small potatoes. Later then, Helen can look after it, she's good at that." I smiled at her. "One of you has to do it all the time and keep track. You know what I mean?"

"Think it over for a few days," I continued finally, because nobody had said anything. "I'd really like to help. You know by now how my inventor mind works; I can't stand still and let things slide by slowly. I like to look ahead and assist in events and happenings. I'm a go-getter in that respect."

Then I said, "The other idea I have is about your vegetable cuttings, the remains left on the field, the stuff you dig under eventually so it'll deteriorate in the soil. But the rotting process takes such a long time. I've a magazine article where it says that it can be done much faster by putting it into a barrel and turning it over twice a week. There are holes in the barrel, of course, to let some air in. You see, that way it might come to good use for a second crop in the same season. I'll let you read the article. You've those big barrels there, after all, given to you for the dripping irrigation at one time, but you never needed them. I've a welder a home to cut some holes into the metal walls. The composting is done considerably faster that way."

Those two suggestions to my neighbor and farmer friend kept me away from my workshop for almost three weeks; that's how busy I was in first getting the ad idea into play and, secondly, cutting, welding and arranging the dozen barrels in the vegetable fields. The huge barrels -- about twelve times the size of oil drums -- sure kept me on the go with the welding torch. Oh, I was so glad that they decided to go through with it, because I strongly believed it would benefit them. It had been the voice from within telling me.

The large ads in the papers were so successful that not even a single vegetable was left on the fields. In fact, the retailers stood in line to be able to lay their hands on the first-rate produce. Once the name Bonson became known, every store selling their vegetables, put the Bonson name up in the produce section and sold out in a jiffy. People were anxious to have the quality vegetables, and the name 'organic' gained its rightful place in many people's minds the first time.

Now they had one of the big barrels on every field to speed up the composting of the vegetable remains, which was quite substantial. Filled, they were much too heavy to turn over by hand, of course, so, twice a week someone took a tractor with a front loader around, to do the job. It worked extremely well and the decomposing material was ready to be used in three to four weeks.

Bill was so happy about it and told me, "Next year we're going to plan right from the beginning for two crops. Boy, Arden, what a marvellous idea and it takes so little time."

I was so happy that it worked out the way it did and that I was able to contribute to my neighbor's organic farm success in a considerable short time. I couldn't help it, but, besides physically, I also was emotionally close to them. How could I let them struggle on their own? We simply meant too much to each other. After all, a deep inner bond was there from way back.

Chapter 20
SOUL IS

When I fell asleep one evening, I immediately became aware of being in the dream state. To my pleasant surprise, the Bonson adults were there, too. I hoped this to happen for a long time; why shouldn't we develop together spiritually, and also have a closer relationship that way.

We were on some part of the vast Astral plane, where people, including us three, were dressed in typical western clothes. Entering a beautiful park, we heard the happy voices of many children and came to a half circle of benches, arranged around a wading pool. When two mothers with their children got up and left, we took their seats and watched the playing youngsters in the water. The atmosphere was relaxed.

There was a discussion about the upbringing of children under-way and, after listening for a while Marg also began to participate in having her say on the subject. Most of the benches could be moved and not too long hence a complete circle had been formed by the listeners. Besides Bill and myself, I saw two other men in our happy group, and particularly the younger one had a few words here and there. The elderly gentleman, around eighty years of age, I judged, sat there with the hands folded in his lap, smiling and nodding. The more often my eyes strayed over to him, the more he fascinated me. I couldn't say what it was; it seemed like an inner magic pull.

I heard Marg say, "Children should have some kind of guidance from their parents; to leave them completely on their own is asking for troubles. A child has to learn the right and wrong from its mother and father. You're right, of course, that Soul is the real being and God-like in nature, but not the body the child is wearing."

I had to scratch my head; was this the Marg speaking I knew as my neighbor? She must be more knowledgeable in spiritual matters than she let on to me. But then it occurred to me that here in the Astral world, wearing our Astral bodies, does not necessarily mean that we have a continuity in awareness to the physical level, the world we live in. In other words, Marg might not be aware of her astral activity while back on the farm. I aimed to find out.

The discussion went on and the young man said, "The best education a parent can give is, if a channel is kept open early in a child's life, like a fine thread between the real being, which is Soul of course, and the present body it must wear. I'm speaking of the brain, the new developing mind. If this connection between Soul and mind is kept open all through childhood and the time of adolescence, a parent has truly succeeded in the ultimate goal of having raised a son or daughter of God. The connection between below and above is always there and never will be broken again."

Beautifully said, I thought, what an advanced Soul he must be. I saw him glancing at the old man, who nodded and smiled back at the young man, who then asked, "Sir, I'm not all-knowing, perhaps you can enlighten us of the supreme path, a way without the many limitations we still have to face in this world."

The elderly gentleman looked around with his glistening eyes, not missing one of the attentive listeners. He began, "You said it so well already, my friend, but as long as we are this form, nothing is ever complete nor can the ultimate goal be achieved and reached." As he looked around again, his smile seemed to have a soothing effect on us all.

"Soul is the real being," he began again. "You all know that and also know that a Godly quality and potential is the divine inheritance of Soul. If we only would stop and think about it for a moment and let the meaning of the foregoing harden into a consciousness so far not realized by some of us.

"God of ITSELF cannot even be imagined in our wildest dreams, IT is too vast, too incomprehensible to our limited minds. However, with our true self, Soul, IT can be contacted as often as we make the effort and take the initiative, if we simply sit still, or lie down and put our attention on the spiritual eye on our forehead above the nose. There lies Soul's door to escape its present vehicle and prison for a moment or two and contact one of God's Agents

140

and divine Messengers, or even be linked up with Spirit, the sustaining power of God. On the other hand, one might attend a comprehensive lecture, travel into the true spiritual worlds, or a message is passed on, vital to the neophyte in his or her spiritual quest. All can be reached; all can be accomplished; Soul is all! SOUL IS!

"Look into the eyes of a new-born or a young child, and you know that it is in contact with God. The soft spot on top of the head is a good indication and proof of Soul's escape from its restricted body. When this spot hardens later on, often that escape is cut off, but it can be reopened again through spiritual exercises and the focus to the spiritual eye on the forehead. A child's mind is not developed enough, of course, to accomplish that.

"However, we as parents can assist our children in that regard and make them aware of this feasibility. Often the old memory comes back and the mind of a child -- not having been programmed yet with the hardened material of an adult -- is only little hindrance for Soul's journey back into its old home of God again.

"The escape from its instrument, the body Soul must wear for a while, is as easy as eating and drinking, but we have to learn to raise our consciousness enough and take the initiative. Often our children are the ones to follow with their child-like attitude and insight many of us matured adults have lost. Remember, Soul is adult during any time of Its journey in the lower worlds, no matter how young the body is It wears."

The discourse had ended and the venerable, elderly gentleman sat back to fold his hands in front of him again, smiling and nodding, as if he was very satisfied with his talk.

All of us listeners sat in deep thought for a while until a few mothers began to attend to their children in the water. We three also got up to slowly continue our walk through the park.

I heard Bill say, "Our children are grown, but its not too late to teach them now."

"What about ourselves, Bill," Marg questioned, "first of all, we have to learn it."

With Marg's last words still audible in my ears I woke up, smiling to myself with deep satisfaction. Tomorrow we three would have something to talk about.

* * *

It was Sunday morning and Willy and I had just finished breakfast. I was thinking about the dream and why the dream Master had put us three together for that experience. Last night I had looked forward to discussing it with Marg and Bill, but in thinking about it now, I wasn't too sure anymore whether the two actually remembered the dream and the discourse of the elderly gentleman, who, I'm quite sure, must have been one of the Masters belonging to the group of Spiritual Adepts I heard mentioned several times.

It would be a day of flying, the weather certainly looked promising. The sun stood unobstructed on the lower sky and it was too early to say whether some cumulus clouds might favor our glider soaring later on.

We two did a few outside chores in the garden and the chicken coop. Then Willy mowed the hill of our flying activity, while I took Jodie for a walk over the fields into the woods. She always seemed to sense when a crowd for flying was to be expected and showed it in her behavior, like a hunting dog who knows beforehand when his master is going hunting.

Suddenly, my pet goat stood still as if it had gotten the wind of something unexpected. I asked quietly, "What is it, Jodie, a deer?"

Slowly and carefully, without making a noise, we walked on. A light wind blew into our direction, so that any wild animal ahead of us would hardly be able to get our scent. Jodie was shaking her head, an indication that she didn't like the smell. Sneaking around a bend of the logging road, exposed a medium-sized bear with its back to us about fifty yards away, eating noisily something I could not identify. We heard it smacking its lips with delight.

Before I could do anything or even think about the situation, Jodie bolted for the bear with the speed of lightning, horns down for the impact. In agony I cried: "Jodie, Jodie, hold it, no, no, Jodie, Jodie!"

It was no good! In my imagination I saw her already mauled half to death and in her blood on the ground with the bear standing on top for the kill. But it didn't happen at all; instead, the bear took to flight, and I mean flight! As if attacked by an animal five times it size. I kept on yelling for my pet, running along the road as fast as I could. I heard the two crashing through the undergrowth and

142

then it was quiet.

A few minutes later, my goat friend came happily out of some bushes, jumping up on her hind legs several times and giving this funny twist with her head, as if to say, "Boy, did I give it to him! Did you see him running? Scared to death."

I just greeted her with a shaking head and suddenly burst out laughing aloud; I simply couldn't hold myself. This was something for a movie! I could see the headline: 'Feisty goat tackles bear with zest, while owner cringes with fear.'

Still chuckling and drying my tears of enjoyment away, we came upon the spot where the bear had feasted; it was a bee's nest and the mad insects still were around and darting for us now. We had to take a quick flight or be stung by the pests. Wow, wait 'til they hear about this experience later on!

On our way back I talked to my beloved pet, telling her that such action, although very courageous, might not be very wise, because bears were very strong and might wipe the wits out of her with one swing of its paw. But, I doubted whether she would listen to me even if she could've grasped my words.

On the other hand, my calling after her and the sudden noise we made, could've chased the bear away. All by herself, Jodie might've acted differently. Or was she trying to protect me? And what about the spiritual angle? Had Soul inspired her? Was all-knowing Spirit responsible for this happening? All those questions turned up in my mind, not finding quick answers.

We all had a good laugh about this event, when I passed it on while moving the gliders on the little hill to get ready for the day.

To get to the bottom of the dream experience and what the two Bonson adults knew about it, I decided to simply ask them. "Did you have a good dream last night, Bill and Marg? Or still nothing?"

Bill made a funny face and answered, "Not that I know of any, did you, Marg?"

"I feel that I dream," she answered with raised shoulders and hands, "but when I wake up, it's wiped out again."

"I'm just asking you two," I said, trying to take the importance out of it. "I wouldn't worry; you'll catch on later, at the right time."

Of course, as Souls they had grasped the so-important discourse by the Master on the Astral plane, but were not yet ready in their present physical awareness to comprehend and analyze it properly. I simply had to get used to the fact that none of us were on the same spiritual level and understanding, and that included my son, Willy. Besides the importance of the discourse, the lesson out of this dream for me was very obvious, namely to stand back and not to interfere. In opening my mouth I could do much harm. After all, individually we're on our own! It's that simple and I would do well to respect it.

There is an old occult law: As above, so below. In other words, the laws of God governing the spiritual worlds are also valid for us here in the physical universe. There are no two ways about it and it's no use to kid ourselves about this fact and be ignorant. But, although parallel, there is a difference between the other worlds and here in the physical; an untrained mind often does not remember the inner experience.

Chapter 21
St. Paul: I Die Daily

It was Christmas Eve and Willy and I had gone down to the Bonsons for dinner, as was our custom every year. Marg never would've forgiven us if we had refused her invitation; besides, we looked very much forward to it. I was sitting in the large living room with Bill and having Roi, Helen's son, on my lap. It was such a mild winter this year and the young people had gone outside for a walk, while the women made the last preparations in the kitchen. We had just finished watching the Country Hour on TV and talked about greenhouse farming we'd seen, something becoming more and more popular here in the northern parts of America.

Although my neighbors had done extremely well this year because of the good weather conditions, there always was the fear in the back of a farmer's mind about too much rain, early frost and a complete wipe-out of his crop. I was so happy that I had been able to contribute somehow to their success, particularly when Bill passed on to me, "You know, Arden, we could pay off half the loan this year because of your ideas, they sure helped a lot. Weather permitting, next year we'll be able to do two crops and put the loan behind us or even save some money for emergencies."

After having shut off the TV, Bill said, "If we had the natural gas they have in Alberta, I might seriously think about starting also a greenhouse and adding one every year. Can you imagine never being influenced by the weather and growing several crops a year? It's a farmer's dream."

I nodded with a smile, not saying anything for a while. However, my mind had been on the subject for months, after having read a couple of articles in one of my magazines. Should I

145

open my mouth again and give my friend a few ideas born of the thoughts romping around my mind?

Well, I did; in putting a follow-up of his words back to him with a question, I asked, "Is it the missing of natural gas that's holding you? This greenhouse 'thing' sure sounds good to me. Something like early retirement from hard labor, if you look forward to that?" Now it was out. Should I have kept quiet rather?

"Well," Bill said, thinking deeply about the matter for a while, "to tell you the truth, I'm not too knowledgeable about it. What do you think?"

"Even without heat, Bill," I stepped with my words into the subject broadside, "it would make you independent from the weather; that alone is an advantage not easily put aside."

Coming back to the TV program, I said, "The watering system they showed is already outdated. In Israel they do the darnedest things today, not only to save water, but also to grow better crops, all without artificial fertilizers. And even that can be improved; I've some very good ideas to do that. It can be done automatically and all one has to do is harvest the crops three or four times a year, besides planting." I grinned rather roguishly.

But Bill had caught on quickly and looked at me with a knowing grin, "Aha, your inventor mind, hey?"

In the meantime the women and the youngsters had begun carrying the food to the table and Marg called out: "Get ready everybody!"

Little Roi had fallen asleep on my knees and Helen said, "I better put him to bed. He has been excited all day and it tired him."

Bill whispered into my ear, "We'll talk about it later, Arden; you probably have some more things up your sleeves, haven't you?"

I just nodded and it delighted my neighbor, so that Marg, who quickly had looked at his face, said, "What have you two been up to? Another big project, hey? As long as it cuts down on the hard work, not that we mind it, do we, you guys?"

In spite of what she just said, I happen to know that Marg longed for easier work, shorter hours and an early retirement with only a little kitchen work. She brought up five children besides doing a lot of farm work from five in the morning to eleven at night. I could 'feel for her' and I sympathized with her having an eye on a rocking chair rather sooner than later.

* * *

It was the first day of spring and the Bonsons were on their way to inspect a greenhouse I had built; it attached to my house for convenience. I always wanted to grow my own vegetables the year round and have a few tropical fruits like figs -- I loved green figs.

It was all automatic and computerised, ready to be demonstrated to my neighbors, so that they could decide whether this was really something they wanted and could afford.

Well, Bill was enthusiastic all right, while Marg thought about another loan they might have to put up with. Finally she said, "If it means early retirement for me, I'm for it."

This time I kept my mouth shut, I simply had to learn not to interfere or to influence their decision, no matter how close I was to the Bonsons and how much I liked and loved them.

Five months later the Bonsons had a brand new greenhouse and I had done much of the inside installations including the computer hook-up. We also had added long rows of solar panels so that they would have enough heat to grow crops during the winter months. This concept was new up here in the north, but I was very confident that it would work.

And work it did! In fact, Bill was talking already about a second greenhouse, but Marg said, with a mellow smile this time, "Come on now, Bill, let's pay off the loan first." She had begun to like the project because the advantages were only too obvious. Wisely enough, I had taught the three Bonson boys much of the greenhouse installations, so that they could do it themselves next time, I hoped.

* * *

Now that my neighbors were occupied with their new inside enterprise and the rest of the farm, I hardly saw them anymore, they simply were too busy. And so was my son with his school work. The only one with me during the day was Jodie, my pet goat, who visited me regularly in the workshop, not so much to see what I was doing, but rather to coax me into a hike with her.

Whatever, my new project didn't want to take shape, I wasn't able to kneel myself into it, so to speak, as I had done with all my other undertakings and inventions. The inner drive simply wasn't there at the moment.

So I found myself walking out with my goat friend more and more and enjoyed it rather. I began to wonder whether I had come to a crossroad in my life? Had my desire to invent dried up?

* * *

During this dream I found myself in a Wisdom Temple, but did not recognize the location. I knew I was in one of the famous spiritual places just by the feel of it -- nowhere else the vibrations are so high. Having been to others before, I knew it only too well.

A guide took me along several corridors into a room, where forty or fifty people already were present. Instead of sitting in tailor fashion on the floor, as I often had done before, we were seated on chairs this time. As far as I could make out, we all might have been several races from our planet Earth.

I knew instantly that he was a Master when our lecturer entered; the shine he brought with him, the feeling he gave me; unerringly, I was at once conscious of his high spiritual status. His eyes glistened like two stars and seemed to stir our insides without any words having come over his lips so far. It was a wonderful experience, an inner action without action. But my description never could replace the personal encounter.

He could've been in his thirties, close to six feet tall. He was clean shaven even on top of his head.

There seemed to come a fine change over his face when he began to speak, which was not in actual words, but rather in vibratory impulses, somewhat like mental telepathy. He said, "The current coming out of the God-head is called Spirit or Holy Spirit and It has all the attributes of God. It is omnipotent, omnipresent, omniscient and therefore the life-giving Force of all the worlds. Without It you and I would not be here and the lower worlds would be devoid of matter and life.

"However, there is another purpose of Spirit, which could be compared with a radio wave going out from its source, the radio station -- God. This purpose is to bring Soul back to its Creator, its old home, the Ocean of Love and Mercy.

"There are two attributes of Spirit important to Soul and they are the Light and Sound of God, also called Bani. On its search for God, Soul should look for the Light and Sound first of all, or it will stay forever in the bowels of the lower worlds.

"Soul can learn to escape its instrument, the body it is wearing at the time, with the assistance of Spirit, and it can do it <u>now</u>. It can learn to ride the Bani out of its present environment into the vast worlds of God and explore its new old home, where it will

148

stay eventually for good as a co-worker with God. However, this will not happen all by itself, the effort has to be made and the initiative be taken.

"Beside Spirit, there are other vehicles for God, equally important to Soul, if not more so, ITS direct Agents. They are still wearing the bodies of the lower worlds, and you can meet them, wherever you live. These Agents of God will assist you in your spiritual search and link you up with the Bani.

"You meet them in your dreams first and as you mature in spiritual knowledge and understanding, they'll teach you to get out of your body and ride on the Bani-current – as Soul, the real you – into the worlds of Spirit and God. This can be done every day, as you advance. St. Paul said: I die daily. The meaning of his words are that, while the body stays behind, Soul can explore the worlds of heaven.

"In your quest for God-realization and an honest desire to reach your old home again, find a Spiritual Voyager, a true Agent of the Supreme Being, and he will first link you up with the Light and Sound of God, and, secondly, assist and guide you to reach that goal. But only genuine love can bring you to that important stage in your life.

"Sit still every day for half an hour in contemplation and do your Spiritual Exercises in putting your attention to the Spiritual Eye on your forehead. Imagine the place of your desire in picture form on the screen of your inner vision as vividly as possible, and not too long hence your imagination will harden into reality. There is nothing mystical about this, in fact, God has given us the faculty of imagination to use as a tool for this purpose."

His eyes had taken on again the star-like vision, as he looked at us, the rows of listeners. I had the distinct impression that he gazed solely at me, but I'm sure that everyone of us had the very same conception.

* * *

Now I knew why my lust for inventions had kind of tapered down; Soul was trying to tell me that I had reached a new stage in my spiritual development. I wanted to be able to leave my physical body consciously in doing Soul Riding, and not just wait until my dream Master would give me the experience. That had been the message of the discourse. I was ready and would implement it at once. A new era in my life had arrived!

Chapter 22
My Last Invention ...

I was so proud of my son; he really had worked hard of his own initiative to finish high school with the boys of his age and he did. It also was graduation time at the Bonsons with Hanna. So we decided to have our party together at their place.

Sometimes I still was thinking about the two, when they first came to my farm and looked through the opening of the workshop door, only eleven years old then, and now they were eighteen already. They always had been inseparable friends and it didn't surprise me at all when they expressed their desire to go to college together and become engineers.

First, we had been to school where the diplomas were handed out and now were assembled in the garden, where Bill and the boys had put up tables and benches for the occasion; the weather was perfect.

I guess I was the only one not to consume any alcohol because of my allergy reaction, but that didn't prevent me from being as happy and having as much fun as the others. At one time I had taken a vow never to touch a drink again out of spiritual reasons, too. In one of my earlier dreams I was made aware of the fact that alcohol inhibits the mind functions to a certain extent, not desirable when contacted by Soul. The same was true for smoking. With all the delicious drinks I was making at home now, there was no reason anyway to indulge in 'firewater' of any kind.

Going on fall and into the winter, I finally was able to finish a prototype of my magnetic train engine, to be run on the narrow track I had purchased two or three years before. However, my heart hadn't been in the venture at all; the old fun was gone. The tracks were grown over by high grass now and couldn't even be seen anymore, but I decided to run it the way it was and simply

150

installed bumper-like edges in front and the back of the engine. That should flatten the grass enough. I had the couldn't-care-less feeling all the time there didn't seem to be any importance in what I was doing.

One thing was for sure, I had to get Jodie out of the way, or she surely might get hurt and be killed. So I put her with some of her favorite food in the stable, to be on the safe side.

I had chosen to have the first run on my own, then if there were any dangerous surprises, nobody else would get injured. Willy was at college anyway, and I hadn't mentioned it to my neighbors, who were busy on their farm. It was much too heavy to carry, so I put copper wires along the ground right up to the tracks, about forty yards away.

The low current I already had applied to the tracks. A large battery in the engine would give me the power for the magnetic field, which was automatically recharged while running.

For the control, I had two levers, one for the creation of the magnetic cushion, and the other one for the forward and backward movements of the vehicle. "Here I go!" I called out loud to myself. There was a certain excitement in my consciousness and it filled the air. Would it work?

A deep sound emanated from the engine, as it lifted off the ground slowly. The control was perfect. Now I led her forward into the direction of the tracks. The floating motion was unbelievably soft, as if running on cotton wool. Having reached the iron rails, I turned it ninety degrees to be in line to the track run. The control, to my utter amazement, was dead accurate; in other words, I had the movements of my brain child in the palm of my hand. Well, this particular part I had done exactly the way I had seen it at the Astral museum in the city of Sahasra-Dal-Kanwal, and now I was glad I did.

I accelerated to a slow speed over the whole length of the rail and back again to the farm yard. The other direction would be three-quarters of a mile down to the Bonson farm and I didn't want them to know yet that I was running it. So I only did the three miles on my property.

This time I ran it faster back and forth a couple of times to a top speed of eighty miles per hour. The distance of the tracks was too limited. I had to relocate them into a circle to really be able to go for higher speeds.

While for a second on the top speed, I suddenly saw Jodie out of the corner of my eyes running toward me, to my surprise and dismay. The only way to avoid a head-on collision was to come to a sudden stop. Pulling the level backwards quickly was the last physical awareness I remember. Almost instantly I hovered above the scene in my astral body and saw the engine stopped with me still inside, slumped over the instrument panel and Jodie crumbled in front of the bumper. We both looked dead all right. That my life should have come to such a quick end, still short of my spiritual goals I had set for myself!

Then I thought about Willy; we had had such a short time to enjoy each other as father and son. Now he was on his own again. And I thought about the Bonsons. Suddenly I saw my pet friend struggling to her feet and walking. Luckily, she only had been stunned. She even put her nose to the partly opened door of the train, and at that moment my body began to stir; I rushed inside to take control. I still was alive!

My head was buzzing and sore and I began to rub my forehead -- it began to swell. I must've hit the dashboard which was not padded as they do our modern cars today. As I slowly began to get my bearings again, the first thoughts coming to mind were that I had better install a seatbelt, including shoulder straps.

When I felt Jodie nuzzling my pants, I was so glad and jumped through the door to put my arms around her, she was alive and well. I invited her inside, but she was very reluctant at first. Then she put her front legs on the dashboard to see what I was doing, while we slowly drove back to the farm buildings where I shut the motor off. In the past few years I always had tried to look behind the scenes of every happening. I believed strongly that nothing ever occurs accidentally. Jodie had been used to give me a message.

My pet goat had found a way to get out of her stable in lifting a piece of plywood and I began to wonder what had taken her so long to find that easy route to freedom. It was something like Soul imprisoned for such a long time, until it really wants to get out. And then, assisted by Spirit, the escape is easy and just happened to come at a certain time. As smart as she was, why had she never tried it before?

This timely accident and experience was, fortunately, a blessing in more ways than one. First, Jodie never ran at the moving train again and only came near it when the motor was shut

152

off. A noise of a high frequency, not detectable by our human ear, she was able to pick up from far away, similar to a dog whistle. Secondly, this whole incident made me aware of the magnetic machine's power, not only to run it with almost unlimited speeds, but also to stop it on a dime, if it wasn't for the gravitational force, which certainly would black me out if I dared to try. It almost killed me now.

* * *

This magnetic force I had created with my machine was exact and powerful, but it also could be dangerous if not kept under tight control, something within the range of today's technology, of course.

However, for some time already I have been aware of the fact that this force or energy is fundamentally the same power used by the space travellers (UFOs), and it's called the cosmic energy. It would not take long for our scientists to figure that one out and its tremendous potential coming with it.

The more I thought about 'my invention', the more the determination crystallized in my mind and heart that this never should get out of my backyard. And I could see it so clearly now that our pet, Jodie, had been a blessing in disguise.

Of course, the benefits to our environment would be overwhelming, not to speak of the revolutionization of the world's railroad systems. Naturally, this propulsion could also be adopted to cars, any time we chose to, with an easy converter to the motor; and that really would cause a revolution in the truest sense of the word. If the rug gets pulled out from underneath big business, a war is in the making. Many people would loose their work; the whole world economy would probably change overnight! And I haven't even begun to mention the war machinery, how this magnetic motor would change its concepts completely. And what about the flights into space? No more rockets, and our solar system becomes too small. What do we know about space ethics? Debris are cluttering the worlds out there now.

Yes, I can hear many thousand voices, all speaking of the benefits and blessings this energy would bring to our world and surely outweigh the negative aspects by a long margin. Most of these people are not rational thinkers and are largely led by their emotions. I honestly wish I could go along with them.

I'm not a person who thrives on negativity and its thoughts

and feelings, in fact, I'm an optimist. But I also have to deal with my intuition and conscience, which is Soul! And from there comes the voice with an unequivocal NO!

* * *

After I had given my son and all the Bonsons several runs, I decided to do one more thing before scrapping it forever, never to be put on the market by me. I wanted to run it continuously, which was only possible in a circle, with the few available rails we had. In that way I was able to accelerate to a high speed.

Because of the winter it took me four months to relocate the tracks in a complete circle on even ground in the back of my farm. I ran the train several times to a speed of two hundred miles per hour. I was afraid to go faster because the darn tracks began to move and could come apart. Besides, my vehicle was not built to lean inside and I was pressed against the side of the cabin and feared to black out and lose consciousness.

When we all sat together later on, Willy said, "Sooner or later somebody is going to invent the same machine, Dad, why not you putting it on the market? I mean, if you yourself don't want to be connected with it, give it to a manufacturer, a responsible outfit. It's such a shame to get rid of it again, after all the work you put into it. And our society will never see the benefit. Look, how much it would cut down on pollution."

"He's got a good point there, Arden," Bill agreed. "It was given to you for a reason in your dream, and not just to fiddle around with it. All your inventions were given to you to be used."

At this point I thought to tell them the whole story of the magnetic motor in the train, that it actually could be converted into utilizing the cosmic energy. I gave them a rough idea what it was and the implications it would cause.

However, Willy insisted I bring it to market for the world's benefit. Finally, Hanna came to my defence, saying, "I wouldn't sell it either. You never did with the Mind Tinkers, and this is much worse, as I see it. I'm with you, Arden. Our world is not ready for this kind of revolutionary invention, they'll get too crazy over it."

With a deep smile I thanked her. There was an advanced Soul. I could see that it would be best not to discuss it any further; our differences were too severe and only would cause emotional and mental pain. Our relationship was too dear to me to be jeopardized

154

by a useless debate. I was disappointed, though, about my son and Bill, both very close to me, that they were not able to rise above the whole situation with emotional detachment.

Little Roi ripped me out of my sadness with the question, "Are you unhappy, Uncle Arden?"

Lifting him up I answered, "No, some sadness got into my head and heart."

"What's sadness?" the child's curiosity inquired.

Spirit used a child as a vehicle to give me an opportunity to explain my feelings over our disagreement we had. It was left to the individual to do their own thorough thinking on the matter.

* * *

In the middle of the night I went out to destroy the magnetic engine, if not the vehicle itself. I wanted it to stay there in the field as a reminder to us all, that there is more to the overall life than physical achievements and satisfaction.

I made up my mind to never invent anything of that nature again. Our world was too materialistic and immature. From now on much of my time and effort I would invest in spiritual matters rather. I had to grin about old Jodie. She almost knocked her brains out to point to the real values of life. I could see the headlines: Goat knocks sense into inventor.

Chapter 23
Let Love in Your Heart Be the Overlord!

Almost one and a half years later and I found myself at odds with life. I'm not sure whether the word odd gives the proper description of my present consciousness, but its the best I can find.

After having stopped my old occupation of inventing, I kind of was in a vacuum on the physical level. I knew very well that going with Jodie for long walks every day and doing a little garden and housework was not the wand I wanted to cling to for the rest of my life.

To my surprise, I came up with an idea, I would've found impossible to even consider only a couple or so years before, and that was writing. Even in my old German language I never felt too comfortable with the pen, and today I was still struggling kind of with the new tongue, so that the difficulties might even double.

Yet, through several dreams and contemplations of what to do with my future, writing, as it was revealed to me, would fit well into the niche I had willingly created. After giving it several tries on my own, one day a page of the daily newspaper stared me in the face; a collection of college curriculum, were offered for a better education and enrichment of life. Immediately, I signed up for the writer's course.

Eight months later I was not a full-fledged novelist, but had learned the fundamentals of the trade and even some tricks; not to forget, my English improved considerably.

In the meantime, my spiritual side also had taken off, so to speak, I was able to Soul Ride at will and could visit the inner worlds or planes with one of the Masters as my guide. It was rather difficult to put these experiences into words because there is nothing in our physical universe to compare it with. And this also was the main reason why I felt so at odds with my life, environment, my son and the Bonsons, not to mention the other people I knew and came in contact with.

Here was something so extraordinary, so beautiful, but hard to put into words, and I couldn't pass it on or discuss it because nobody I knew was there with me. Besides, I had to observe the law of silence because it was not for me to circulate the spiritual knowledge I had obtained indiscriminately, not even to my beloved ones. At one time I had hoped that Willy and the Bonsons would show enough interest in dreams, reincarnation, karma and the law of cause and effect to follow it through and join me. But they seemed to have lost interest and I had to back off again. All by myself, however, I felt lonely.

It's something like a young boy who climbs a high mountain close to his home from where he has the most marvellous sight in all directions, but nobody is interested in following him and seeing for themselves. After telling his parents first and seeing their doubtful eyes, he becomes very quiet and withdrawn.

As an adult, though, my reaction was different because I was able to cope with the situation emotionally. The relationship with my close ones did not deteriorate and only I was aware of a change, and a feeling of sadness crept into me at times. My priorities had changed dramatically while theirs were still the same. Even my heart and love felt strange; they were more refined and purer.

This is not to air my complaints in any way, but to explain why I'm at odds with life in more ways than one. There were times when I was longing for somebody I'm close to, or know, to come with me into the other worlds. Why can't we share in the same spiritual undertakings? I know of course, it's because of our different karma. Yet we all had been together so often in past reincarnations with the same experiences, why not in this last struggle for liberation? This question ran through my mind many times, and it didn't want to die down because I was lonely on my own.

* * *

One night my old dream Master met me somewhere on the Astral plane on top of a high plateau from where we could see into the far distances of this world. He said, "You know already that individually you're on your own; no two are on the same stage of

157

their spiritual development.

"See the many and uncounted people down there? See all the different lifetimes they have to go through? It's not just for a few hundred years, but it goes into the millions."

Something like a huge movie picture was running past me, created by my guide for my benefit. Although the contents of the illustration were vast, I was able to recognize individual scenes and I watched them with intensity because they were so interesting.

"Here, have a close look at several of your lives. You came to the planet Earth thirty thousand years ago and began with Atlantis, where you had several incarnations."

None of the people I was together with in any of those lives did I recognize with the exception of my former wife. Then I was shown several lives in China and India; it must have been six or seven thousand years ago, but I didn't recognize anybody of today. Old Egypt, Greece, France, England and back to France again, where I finally recognized Willy as my brother. From that period on, I incarnated through different European countries and was joined by the Bonsons in England (Chapter 7, The Mind Tinkers), my ex-wife and daughters in Spain and Italy.

They were the Medieval times, and only from there on the Bonsons, Willy, my ex-wife, daughters and my old relatives from Germany, including my parents, began spending lifetimes with me, on and off, in different positions, but also sexes. I heard the voice of my dream Friend say, "You, see, that time span is a very small portion of all the lives you've ever lived. It just so happened that karma brought some of the old actors together again in your present life, which does not mean at all that everyone has the same maturity as Soul. If you're brought together in this life, it might be for the purpose of learning an old lesson you couldn't cope with before.

"All this is so precise that nothing is left out under the eternal plan, but the freedom of choice of the individual is a force not to ignore and not even God will interfere with it.

"It stands to reason that in the many lifetimes involved, not very often two Souls succeed in getting to the same plateau of understanding, and being together again in one particular life does not mean that either.

"The high path of spiritual attainment is a lonely one when the loved ones stay behind. However, look at the rewards; the blessings of the Most High can be felt all the time and be seen and heard as Light and Sound. Can there be more enlightenment than that?"

The play of the mammoth movie had ended and we two walked on the bare rock of the plateau around for a while until he spoke once more. "The planet Earth is heading for a giant spiritual awakening and your people will make a big leap toward God-realization and the way back to their old home of Love and Mercy. Your consciousness already has changed way ahead of your fellow men. Your old likes have dried up like a mud puddle and the spring of spirituality becomes stronger with every new recognition. Spirit has initiated a tool in you to become a vehicle for Its Godly message. Although still in its infancy at this time, that instrument will become a powerful mouthpiece and channel eventually for its Originator.

"Whatever you do, let love in your heart be the overlord of all your undertakings and nothing will go wrong because God of ITSELF is the guide. Always remember that."

* * *

I woke up in bed with the words: "Always remember that." This would be baked into my consciousness from there on.

This dream had a tremendous sobering effect on me. To begin with, I stopped feeling sorry for myself. Yes, that's what I had done. Being lonely is often born of the foregoing; it certainly was in my case. So I straightened out once and for all and got rid of self pity.

Naturally, with the many lifetimes involved, only considering the reincarnations on Earth -- there had been millions more on other planets and in the spiritual world also -- no two Souls would reach the same stepping stone on their spiritual ladder. So I had to learn to live with my son and the Bonsons the way they were. I was not Spirit nor God to "turn them on", so to speak, but I could be a channel for both and perhaps something might develop right under my nose eventually, if I give them their rightful freedom of choice.

The other important message out of the dream was, of course, that writing would be my future life, a tool for Spirit and a co-worker with God. And how could I forget the last words of my dream Friend, the advice that love should always be my guide. I shall let it flow through my pen.

159

Chapter 24
The "Secret" Name of God ...

Three weeks later, it was a Sunday afternoon and Jodie waited for me to go on a little hike. Willy had left early to meet his college friends. There were not many weekends anymore when he stayed around to relax or have a chat with me. But I wasn't worried about him; he and Hanna were very strong characters and spent most of the time together.

As I led my pet goat into the field toward the woods, I thought I heard a car approaching and turned around to see. It was Willy and I began to wonder what the unusual occasion might be. "Come on, Jodie, Willy just drove up, let's see what's on his mind," I coaxed her to go back. We two walked toward the house and, to my surprise, I also was greeted by Hanna.

After they both had romped around with Jodie for a while, Willy asked, "You think, Dad, we could have a talk with you? Don't worry, it's nothing ... well, I'm not in trouble or anything."

"Okay, you two," I smiled with relief, "shall we walk around outside? I must admit, you're a Sunday afternoon surprise to me. When did I ever see you guys stick around for a day lately. I'm not complaining, mind you, but at times one can't help thinking of the past when you were anxious to stay with me, and our weekends were events with flying and fun in the sky," I laughed.

"You still did a lot of inventing then, too," Willy burst out, "but today ..." he trailed off.

"But today?" I put the question back to him.

"Well, the flying is very seasonal, and what else can we do?" he said seriously. "Look, Dad, we're grown now and are ... and want more out of life. It has to be attractive. We can't just sit

160

around here all day and do nothing. You have your writing now, but we, well, it takes a long time to get going and sell a novel. Besides, we can't have any part in that."

I didn't want to rebut his words; obviously, they were not too sure what to say or how to begin. I was surprised that Hanna was so quiet. I didn't answer and suddenly felt her arm hooking into mine. Our eyes met for a moment and hers said, 'We're here now, Arden.'

"Well, what made you come up today?" I grinned and continued, "an old longing for the old times? Since I haven't got much to offer now?"

"Hanna and I talked about all this and, yes, about you, too," Willy said with a faint grin. "In any case, we thought that you just don't stop something; it's simply not you, Dad. I was thinking about our disagreement on the magnetic train and what to do with it. It surprised me that you destroyed it so quickly. Maybe there is more to it than you wanted to let on to us?"

Now I lit up inside. Did they come to know more? I waited for him to continue.

My son had found a flat stone and flipped it over the water of the pond. He asked, "Can we go for a boat ride, Dad?"

"But of course," I answered, "You don't have to ask me that. I'll get us three pillows from the shed. If we sit in there all afternoon," I grinned.

I noticed Jodie's sad look when we three entered the boat, she was left out and didn't like it one bit. So I called to her, "We're going later on, old girl, don't worry."

Hanna asked, "Can I do the rowing?" I think she wanted to face me, having taken a seat in the back.

Gliding slowly over the water seemed to relax us more and for a while nothing was said.

Suddenly Hanna began to speak, "We want to join you again, Arden. We don't believe that you're just writing, going out with Jodie and all that. You do more, far more than that, but you keep it from us, don't you? You might think we're not interested, and maybe we weren't until a few weeks ago when all of us met at our place. Mom and Dad said that it was not like you at all and we should find out. Maybe we can be the old bunch again and do things together." She wasn't too comfortable with her words, I could see that.

Patting her on one hand and grinning in my usual way, I said, "One thing is for sure, you guys; we never will be the old ones again and do things together as we used to. This is not just a physical matter one picks up once more and continues as we did in the olden days. No, it is much vaster than that, much vaster and pretty near inconceivable to the untrained human mind."

At once I heard Willy from the front, "I knew it ... you are involved in something else, I simply knew it."

"We're living under the same roof, son," I answered "and you didn't even once inquire. Have we grown apart to that extent? At one time I honestly believed that at least you two would join me in this venture, which is of a spiritual nature. Remember the dream books? What happened to them?"

A bit later I said, "You see, at that time you lost interest because not much was going on in your dreams. Besides, schools, college, new friends and a new life was waiting away from here. How can I say anything about that? All young people must have their own experiences and only that counts, not what's coming out of a father's mouth. I know that now and I'm still learning. But then I was ... well, not disappointed, but sad."

I was groping for the right words. "In the meantime I've learned a lot," I continued. "The most important thing is to never interfere with somebody's consciousness no matter how close that person might be to you. I was tempted at times, though. So I stopped talking to you about spiritual matters; you had to inquire again out of your own initiative, and perhaps this is the day for a new beginning. However, you must realize that this is not something to be had overnight. And first of all, you really must want it and not to do me a favor or for other physical reasons. The voice from within, remember? Soul must be the initiator."

"What about your parents, Helen and your brothers?" I asked. "Are they all in this, too, and want to hear what quiet, old Arden has up his sleeve this time?" I laughed

Hanna laughed back and answered, "We actually don't know that, Arden, we just wondered about you and talked. But Willy and I are definitely interested."

"All right, you guys," I said, "do remember, however, that I pass this teaching on to you in confidence, and parents, brothers and sister don't matter in this case, unless they ask for it; so you have to keep quiet. It's a spiritual law."

162

Willy had brought out a blanket and we sat down in the grass in front of the house where I began my lecture, the first of many, eventually.

I was so pleased that it had come to this, and certainly had the ears of my young listeners all the way. I learned a lot, too, about young people, what made them 'click'. Of course, they had to have some experiences away from their home environment first, and that made them more so ready for this moment.

* * *

While Soul Riding one night, my Spiritual Guide said, "Tonight we are going to the Wisdom Temple in the city of Retz, the capital of Venus. Two young friends will join you there. An old dream Friend of yours will speak about God."

When I entered the room where he had brought me, Willy and Hanna were seated already with fifteen others on cushions in tailor fashion and greeted me with surprise and grins. The Master entered; he was one of my earliest dream Guides. Soon thereafter he began to speak.

"God has many names and there are many gods, but only one Supreme Being. Every world and plane has a ruler or lord, called god by his followers, who believe him to be the Most High. But they are blinded by ignorance and illusions put before them by the master of deception, Kal Niranjan, the overlord of the lower universes, the worlds of duality. It's his job to keep Soul away from its old home, the Ocean of Love and Mercy. Eventually, only the strongest Soul will break away from the pseudo teachings and the lower world religions, created for man's comfort alone and dear needs.

"But they teach nothing about the Sound and Light of God coming by way of Spirit or Holy Spirit into the lower creation. Riding along this God Current is the only way for Soul to get out of its entrapment of the worlds of duality. However, a link-up has to be made first.

"Often in your dreams you meet a Guide, an instructor or teacher, or you only hear words of advice without seeing anyone. These Beings are Masters, dream Masters, as some of you call them, belonging to a high Spiritual Order, and they will do the link up with Spirit. The head of this Order is the Godman, Light-Giver, Vi-Guru, Sat-Guru and other names he is known under. He is the direct manifestation of the Supreme Lord.

163

"As said in the beginning, there are many gods you'll meet on your spiritual quest for the ultimate realization, all of them claiming that only they know the truth and are the real Supreme Lord. For the neophyte it is often very confusing and difficult to distinguish between real and pseudo. However, there is one sure way to wipe the negative perpetrator out of your dream and mind's vision and that is to call on the Supreme Deity, whose secret name is HU. Most of nature's creatures know this name and use it frequently. You can hear it in the song of a bird, for instance.

"Use it everywhere and anytime, when in fear, when attacked, threatened, when in an accident or when you want spiritual help and God's closeness. Simply sing the word HU as much as you like and help might be on the way sooner than you think, whether you realize, feel it or not. Sing it in a long drawn out HUUUUUUU.

"I called it the secret name of God, which it actually isn't anymore. Your Earth world has reached a new spiritual beginning, not recognized by most of your fellow men. The singing or chanting of the HU can vastly contribute to your uplifting. I have ended"

While Willy and Hanna already had faded out of my sight and out of their own dream state, no doubt, back into the awareness of being in bed, I decided to walk around the Wisdom Temple and do a little exploring. In doing Soul Riding I was on my own and had control over what I was doing. Suddenly the Master who had brought me here appeared with a faint grin and said, "Any other time would be all right to stay for a while and look around, but two young people are anxious at the moment to speak with you of their dream experience. They are knocking on your bedroom door."

On the flip of a finger I was back in my body, just in time to see the door open slowly and two faces looking through the opening. A flashlight shone into my face and, opening my eyes, I said, grinning, "Something is telling me that you two have had the most marvellous dream. I was there, too, you know."

With a wave of my hand I invited them to sit on my bed. They both rushed in and began singing the long drawn-out HUUUUUUUUUU. I was overjoyed. So quickly it had come to this ... Happily I joined in.

END

164

ISBN 155212919-5

9 781552 129197